SIZWE BANSI IS DEAD
and
THE ISLAND

SIZWE BANSI IS DEAD
and
THE ISLAND

by
Athol Fugard
John Kani
and
Winston Ntshona

THE VIKING PRESS NEW YORK

Copyright © 1973, 1974 by Athol Fugard,
John Kani, and Winston Ntshona
All rights reserved
Published in 1976 by The Viking Press
625 Madison Avenue, New York, N.Y. 10022
Published simultaneously in Canada by
The Macmillan Company of Canada Limited

Library of Congress Cataloging in Publication Data
Fugard, Athol.
Sizwe Bansi is dead and The island.
Plays.
I. Kani, John, joint author.
II. Ntshona, Winston, joint author. III. Title.
PR9369.3.F8S5 1976   822   75-45066
ISBN 0-670-64784-5

Printed in U.S.A.

Photographs by William L. Smith

CONTENTS

SIZWE BANSI IS DEAD

CHARACTERS

Styles
Sizwe Bansi
Buntu

This play was given its first performance on 8 October 1972 at The Space, Cape Town, and was directed by Athol Fugard with the following cast:

| Styles and Buntu | John Kani |
| Sizwe Bansi | Winston Ntshona |

John Kani as Styles.

Styles's Photographic Studio in the African township of New Brighton,
Port Elizabeth. Positioned prominently, the name-board:

> *Styles Photographic Studio. Reference Books; Passports;*
> *Weddings; Engagements; Birthday Parties and Parties.*
> *Prop.—Styles.*

Underneath this a display of photographs of various sizes. Centre stage,
a table and chair. This is obviously used for photographs because a camera
on a tripod stands ready a short distance away.

There is also another table, or desk, with odds and ends of photographic
equipment and an assortment of 'props' for photographs.

The setting for this and subsequent scenes should be as simple as
possible so that the action can be continuous.

Styles *walks on with a newspaper. A dapper, alert young man*
wearing a white dustcoat and bowtie. He sits down at the table and starts
to read the paper.

STYLES [*reading the headlines*]. 'Storm buffets Natal. Damage in
many areas . . . trees snapped like . . . what? . . . matchsticks. . . .'

[*He laughs.*]

They're having it, boy! And I'm watching it . . . in the paper.

[*Turning the page, another headline.*]

'China: A question-mark on South West Africa.' What's
China want there? *Yo!* They better be careful. China gets in
there . . . ! [*Laugh.*] I'll tell you what happens . . . .

[*Stops abruptly. Looks around as if someone might be eavesdropping on*
his intimacy with the audience.]

No comment.

[*Back to his paper.*]

What's this? . . . *Ag!* American politics. Nixon and all his
votes. Means buggerall to us.

[*Another page, another headline.*]

'Car plant expansion. 1·5 million rand plan.' *Ja.* I'll tell you
what *that* means . . . more machines, bigger buildings . . . never
any expansion to the pay-packet. Makes me fed-up. I know
what I'm talking about. I worked at Ford one time. We used

3

to read in the newspaper . . . big headlines! . . . 'So and so from America or London made a big speech: ". . . going to see to it that the conditions of their non-white workers in Southern Africa were substantially improved."' The talk ended in the bloody newspaper. Never in the pay-packet.

Another time we read: Mr Henry Ford Junior Number two or whatever the hell he is . . . is visiting the Ford Factories in South Africa!

[*Shakes his head ruefully at the memory.*]

Big news for us, man! When a big man like that visited the plant there was usually a few cents more in the pay-packet at the end of the week.

Ja, a Thursday morning. I walked into the plant . . . 'Hey! What's this?' . . . Everything was quiet! Those big bloody machines that used to make so much noise made my head go around . . . ? Silent! Went to the notice-board and read: Mr Ford's visit today!

The one in charge of us . . . [*laugh*] hey! I remember him. General Foreman Mr 'Baas' Bradley. Good man that one, if you knew how to handle him . . . he called us all together:

[*Styles mimics Mr 'Baas' Bradley. A heavy Afrikaans accent.*]

'Listen, boys, don't go to work on the line. There is going to be a General Cleaning first.'

I used to like General Cleaning. Nothing specific, you know, little bit here, little bit there. But that day! Yessus . . . in came the big machines with hot water and brushes—sort of electric mop—and God alone knows what else. We started on the floors. The oil and dirt under the machines was thick, man. All the time the bosses were walking around watching us:

[*Slapping his hands together as he urges on the 'boys'.*]

'Come on, boys! It's got to be spotless! Big day for the plant!' Even the *big* boss, the one we only used to see lunch-times, walking to the canteen with a big cigar in his mouth and his hands in his pocket . . . that day? Sleeves rolled up, running around us:

'Come on! Spotless, my boys! Over there, John. . . .' I thought: What the hell is happening? It was beginning to feel like hard work, man. I'm telling you we cleaned that place—

spot-checked after fifteen minutes! . . . like you would have thought it had just been built.

First stage of General Cleaning finished. We started on the second. Mr 'Baas' Bradley came in with paint and brushes. I watched.

W—h—i—t—e   l—i—n—e

[*Mr 'Baas' Bradley paints a long white line on the floor.*]

What's this? Been here five years and I never seen a white line before. Then:

[*Mr 'Baas' Bradley at work with the paint-brush.*]

CAREFUL THIS SIDE. TOW MOTOR IN MOTION.

[*Styles laughs.*]

It was nice, man. Safety-precautions after six years. Then another gallon of paint.

Y—e—l—l—o—w   l—i—n—e—

NO SMOKING IN THIS AREA. DANGER!

Then another gallon:

G—r—e—e—n   l—i—n—e—

I noticed that that line cut off the roughcasting section, where we worked with the rough engine blocks as we got them from Iscor. Dangerous world that. Big machines! One mistake there and you're in trouble. I watched them and thought: What's going to happen here? When the green line was finished, down they went on the floor—Mr 'Baas' Bradley, the lot!— with a big green board, a little brush, and a tin of white paint. EYE PROTECTION AREA. Then my big moment:

'Styles!'

'Yes, sir!'

[*Mr 'Baas' Bradley's heavy Afrikaans accent*] 'What do you say in your language for this? Eye Protection Area.'

It was easy, man!

'*Gqokra Izi Khuselo Zamehlo Kule Ndawo.*'

Nobody wrote it!

'Don't bloody fool me, Styles!'

'No, sir!'

'Then spell it . . . slowly.'

[*Styles has a big laugh.*]

Hey! That was my moment, man. Kneeling there on the

floor . . . foreman, general foreman, plant supervisor, plant manager . . . and Styles? Standing!

[*Folds his arms as he acts out his part to the imaginary figures crouched on the floor.*]

'G—q—o—k—r—a' . . . and on I went, with Mr 'Baas' Bradley painting and saying as he wiped away the sweat: 'You're not fooling me, hey!'

After that the green board went up. We all stood and admired it. Plant was looking nice, man! Colourful!

Into the third phase of General Cleaning.

'Styles!'

'Yes, sir!'

'Tell all the boys they must now go to the bathroom and wash themselves clean.'

We needed it! Into the bathroom, under the showers . . . hot water, soap . . . on a Thursday! Before ten? *Yo!* What's happening in the plant? The other chaps asked me: What's going on, Styles? I told them: 'Big-shot cunt from America coming to visit you.' When we finished washing they gave us towels . . . [*laugh*].

Three hundred of us, man! We were so clean we felt shy! Stand there like little ladies in front of the mirror. From there to the General Store.

Handed in my dirty overall.

'Throw it on the floor.'

'Yes, sir!'

New overall comes, wrapped in plastic. Brand new, man! I normally take a thirty-eight but this one was a forty-two. Then next door to the tool room . . . brand new tool bag, set of spanners, shifting spanner, torque wrench—all of them brand new—and because I worked in the dangerous hot test section I was also given a new asbestos apron and fire-proof gloves to replace the ones I had lost about a year ago. I'm telling you I walked back heavy to my spot. Armstrong on the moon! Inside the plant it was general meeting again. General Foreman Mr 'Baas' Bradley called me.

'Styles!'

'Yes, sir.'

'Come translate.'

'Yes, sir!'

[*Styles pulls out a chair. Mr 'Baas' Bradley speaks on one side, Styles translates on the other.*]

'Tell the boys in your language, that this is a very big day in their lives.'

'Gentlemen, this old fool says this is a hell of a big day in our lives.'

The men laughed.

'They are very happy to hear that, sir.'

'Tell the boys that Mr Henry Ford the Second, the owner of this place, is going to visit us. Tell them Mr Ford is the big Baas. He owns the plant and everything in it.'

'Gentlemen, old Bradley says this Ford is a big bastard. He owns everything in this building, which means you as well.'

A voice came out of the crowd:

'Is he a bigger fool than Bradley?'

'They're asking, sir, is he bigger than you?'

'Certainly . . . [*blustering*] . . . certainly. He is a very big baas. He's a . . . [*groping for words*] . . . he's a Makulu Baas.'

I loved that one!

'Mr "Baas" Bradley says most certainly Mr Ford is bigger than him. In fact Mr Ford is the grandmother baas of them all . . . that's what he said to me.'

'Styles, tell the boys that when Mr Henry Ford comes into the plant I want them all to look happy. We will slow down the speed of the line so that they can sing and smile while they are working.'

'Gentlemen, he says that when the door opens and his grandmother walks in you must see to it that you are wearing a mask of smiles. Hide your true feelings, brothers. You must sing. The joyous songs of the days of old before we had fools like this one next to me to worry about.' [*To Bradley.*] 'Yes, sir!'

'Say to them, Styles, that they must try to impress Mr Henry Ford that they are better than those monkeys in his own country, those niggers in Harlem who know nothing but strike, strike.'

Yo! I liked that one too.

'Gentlemen, he says we must remember, when Mr Ford walks in, that we are South African monkeys, not American monkeys. South African monkeys are much better trained. . . .'

Before I could even finish, a voice was shouting out of the crowd:

'He's talking shit!' I had to be careful!

[*Servile and full of smiles as he turns back to Bradley.*]

'No, sir! The men say they are much too happy to behave like those American monkeys.'

Right! Line was switched on nice and slow—and we started working.

[*At work on the Assembly Line; singing.*]

'*Tshotsholoza . . . Tshotsholoza . . . kulezondawo. . . .*'

We had all the time in the world, man! . . . torque wrench out . . . tighten the cylinder-head nut . . . wait for the next one. . . . [*Singing*] '*Vyabaleka . . . vyabaleka . . . kulezondawo. . . .*'

I kept my eye on the front office. I could see them—Mr 'Baas' Bradley, the line supervisor—through the big glass window, brushing their hair, straightening the tie. There was some General Cleaning going on there too.

[*He laughs.*]

We were watching them. Nobody was watching us. Even the old Security Guard. The one who every time he saw a black man walk past with his hands in his pockets he saw another spark-plug walk out of the plant. Today? To hell and gone there on the other side polishing his black shoes.

Then, through the window, I saw three long black Galaxies zoom up. I passed the word down the line: He's come!

Let me tell you what happened. The big doors opened; next thing the General Superintendent, Line Supervisor, General Foreman, Manager, Senior Manager, Managing Director . . . the bloody lot were there . . . like a pack of puppies!

[*Mimics a lot of fawning men retreating before an important person.*]

I looked and laughed! 'Yessus, Styles, they're all playing your part today!' They ran, man! In came a tall man, six foot six, hefty, full of respect and dignity . . . I marvelled at him! Let me show you what he did.

[*Three enormous strides*] One . . . two . . . three. . . . [*Cursory look around as he turns and takes the same three strides back.*]

One . . . two . . . three . . . OUT! Into the Galaxie and gone! That's all. Didn't talk to me, Mr 'Baas' Bradley, Line

Supervisor, or anybody. He didn't even look at the plant! And what did I see when those three Galaxies disappeared? The white staff at the main switchboard.
'Double speed on the line! Make up for production lost!'
It ended up with us working harder that bloody day than ever before. Just because that big. . . . [*shakes his head.*]
Six years there. Six years a bloody fool.

[*Back to his newspaper. A few more headlines with appropriate comment, then. . . .*]

[*Reading*] 'The Mass Murderer! Doom!'

[*Smile of recognition.*]

'For fleas . . . Doom. Flies . . . Doom. Bedbugs . . . Doom. For cockroaches and other household pests. The household insecticide . . . Doom.' Useful stuff. Remember, Styles? *Ja.*

[*To the audience.*] After all that time at Ford I sat down one day. I said to myself:
'Styles, you're a bloody monkey, boy!'
'What do you mean?'
'You're a monkey, man.'
'Go to hell!'
'Come on, Styles, you're a monkey, man, and you know it. Run up and down the whole bloody day! Your life doesn't belong to you. You've sold it. For what, Styles? Gold wrist-watch in twenty-five years time when they sign you off because you're too old for anything any more?'
I was right. I took a good look at my life. What did I see? A bloody circus monkey! Selling most of his time on this earth to another man. Out of every twenty-four hours I could only properly call mine the six when I was sleeping. What the hell is the use of that?
Think about it, friend. Wake up in the morning, half-past six, out of the pyjamas and into the bath-tub, put on your shirt with one hand, socks with the other, realize you got your shoes on the wrong bloody feet, and all the time the seconds are passing and if you don't hurry up you'll miss the bus. . . .
'Get the lunch, dear. I'm late. My lunch, please, darling! . . . then the children come in . . . 'Daddy, can I have this? Daddy, I want money for that.' 'Go to your mother. I haven't got time. Look after the children, please, sweetheart!!'

. . . grab your lunch . . . 'Bye Bye!!' and then run like I-don't-know-what for the bus stop. You call that living? I went back to myself for another chat:

'Suppose you're right. What then?'

'Try something else.'

'Like what?'

Silly question to ask. I knew what I was going to say. Photographer! It was my hobby in those days. I used to pick up a few cents on the side taking cards at parties, weddings, big occasions. But when it came to telling my wife and parents that I wanted to turn professional . . . !!

My father was the worst.

'You call that work? Click-click with a camera. Are you mad?'

I tried to explain. 'Daddy, if I could stand on my own two feet and not be somebody else's tool, I'd have some respect for myself. I'd be a man.'

'What do you mean? Aren't you one already? You're circumcised, you've got a wife. . . .'

Talk about the generation gap!

Anyway I thought: To hell with them. I'm trying it.

It was the Christmas shutdown, so I had lots of time to look around for a studio. My friend Dhlamini at the Funeral Parlour told me about a vacant room next door. He encouraged me. I remember his words. 'Grab your chance, Styles. Grab it before somebody in my line puts you in a box and closes the lid.' I applied for permission to use the room as a studio. After some time the first letter back:

'Your application has been received and is being considered.' A month later: 'The matter is receiving the serious consideration of the Board.' Another month: 'Your application is now on the director's table.' I nearly gave up, friends. But one day, a knock at the door—the postman—I had to sign for a registered letter. 'We are pleased to inform you. . . .'

[*Styles has a good laugh.*]

I ran all the way to the Administration Offices, grabbed the key, ran all the way back to Red Location, unlocked the door, and walked in!

What I found sobered me up a little bit. Window panes were all broken; big hole in the roof, cobwebs in the corners. I didn't let that put me off though. Said to myself: 'This is your chance, Styles. Grab it.' Some kids helped me clean it out. The dust! *Yo!* When the broom walked in the Sahara Desert walked out! But at the end of that day it was reasonably clean. I stood here in the middle of the floor, straight! You know what that means? To stand straight in a place of your own? To be your own . . . General Foreman, Mr 'Baas', Line Supervisor—the lot! I was tall, six foot six and doing my own inspection of the plant.

So I'm standing there—here—feeling big and what do I see on the walls? Cockroaches. *Ja*, cockroaches . . . in *my* place. I don't mean those little things that run all over the place when you pull out the kitchen drawer. I'm talking about the big bastards, the paratroopers as we call them. I didn't like them. I'm not afraid of them but I just don't like them! All over. On the floors, the walls. I heard the one on the wall say: 'What's going on? Who opened the door?' The one on the floor answered: 'Relax. He won't last. This place is condemned.' That's when I thought: Doom.

Out of here and into the Chinaman's shop. 'Good day, sir. I've got a problem. Cockroaches.'

The Chinaman didn't even think, man, he just said: 'Doom!' I said: 'Certainly.' He said: 'Doom, seventy-five cents a tin.' Paid him for two and went back. *Yo!* You should have seen me! Two-tin Charlie!

[*His two tins at the ready, forefingers on the press-buttons, Styles gives us a graphic re-enactment of what happened. There is a brief respite to 'reload'—shake the tins—and tie a handkerchief around his nose after which he returns to the fight. Styles eventually backs through the imaginary door, still firing, and closes it. Spins the tins and puts them into their holsters.*]

I went home to sleep. *I* went to sleep. Not them [*the cockroaches*]. What do you think happened here? General meeting under the floorboards. All the bloody survivors. The old professor addressed them: 'Brothers, we face a problem of serious pollution . . . contamination! The menace appears to be called Doom. I have recommended a general inoculation of the whole community. Everybody in line, please. [*Inoculation proceeds.*] Next . . . next . . . next. . . .' While poor old Styles is

11

smiling in his sleep! Next morning I walked in. . . . [*He stops abruptly.*] . . . What's this? Cockroach walking on the floor? Another one on the ceiling? Not a damn! Doom did it yesterday. Doom does it today. [*Whips out the two tins and goes in fighting. This time, however, it is not long before they peter out.*] Pssssssss . . . pssssss . . . psssss . . . pss [*a last desperate shake, but he barely manages to get out a squirt*].
Pss.

No bloody good! The old bastard on the floor just waved his feelers in the air as if he was enjoying air-conditioning.

I went next door to Dhlamini and told him about my problem. He laughed. 'Doom? You're wasting your time, Styles. You want to solve your problem, get a cat. What do you think a cat lives on in the township? Milk? If there's any the baby gets it. Meat? When the family sees it only once a week? Mice? The little boys got rid of them years ago. Insects, man, township cats are insect-eaters. Here. . . .'

He gave me a little cat. I'm . . . I'm not too fond of cats normally. This one was called Blackie . . . I wasn't too fond of that name either. But . . . Kitsy! Kitsy! Kitsy . . . little Blackie followed me back to the studio.

The next morning when I walked in what do you think I saw? Wings. I smiled. Because one thing I do know is that no cockroach can take his wings off. He's dead!

[*Proud gesture taking in the whole of his studio.*]
So here it is!

[*To his name-board.*]

'Styles Photographic Studio. Reference Books; Passports; Weddings; Engagements; Birthday Parties and Parties. Proprietor: Styles.'

When you look at this, what do you see? Just another photographic studio? Where people come because they've lost their Reference Book and need a photo for the new one? That I sit them down, set up the camera . . . 'No expression, please.' . . . click-click . . . 'Come back tomorrow, please' . . . and then kick them out and wait for the next? No, friend. It's more than just that. This is a strong-room of dreams. The dreamers? My people. The simple people, who you never find mentioned in the history books, who never get statues erected to them, or monuments commemorating their great deeds. People who would be forgotten, and their dreams with them, if it wasn't for Styles. That's what I do, friends. Put down, in my way, on paper the dreams and hopes of my people so that even their children's children will remember a man . . . 'This was our Grandfather' . . . and say his name. Walk into the houses of New Brighton and on the walls you'll find hanging the story of the people the writers of the big books forget about.

[*To his display-board.*]

This one [*a photograph*] walked in here one morning. I was just passing the time. Midweek. Business is always slow then. Anyway, a knock at the door. Yes! I must explain something. I get two types of knock here. When I hear . . . [*knocks solemnly on the table*] . . . I don't even look up, man. 'Funeral parlour is next door.' But when I hear . . . [*energetic rap on the table . . . he laughs*] . . . that's *my* sound, and I shout 'Come in!'

In walked a chap, full of smiles, little parcel under his arm. I can still see him, man!

[*Styles acts both roles.*]

'Mr Styles?'
I said: 'Come in!'
'Mr Styles, I've come to take a snap, Mr Styles.'
I said: 'Sit down! Sit down, my friend!'
'No, Mr Styles. I want to take the snap standing. [*Barely containing his suppressed excitement and happiness*] Mr Styles, take the card, please!'
I said: 'Certainly, friend.'

Something you mustn't do is interfere with a man's dream. If he wants to do it standing, let him stand. If he wants to sit, let him sit. Do exactly what they want! Sometimes they come in here, all smart in a suit, then off comes the jacket and shoes and socks . . . [*adopts a boxer's stance*] . . . 'Take it, Mr Styles. Take it!' And I take it. No questions! Start asking stupid questions and you destroy that dream. Anyway, this chap I'm telling you about . . . [*laughing warmly as he remembers*] . . . I've seen a lot of smiles in my business, friends, but that one gets first prize. I set up my camera, and just as I was ready

13

to go . . . 'Wait, wait, Mr Styles! I want you to take the card with this.' Out of his parcel came a long piece of white paper . . . looked like some sort of document . . . he held it in front of him. [*Styles demonstrates.*] For once I didn't have to say, 'Smile!' Just: 'Hold it!' . . . and, click, . . . finished. I asked him what the document was.

'You see, Mr Styles, I'm forty-eight years old. I work twenty-two years for the municipality and the foreman kept on saying to me if I want promotion to Boss-boy I must try to better my education. I didn't write well, Mr Styles. So I took a course with the Damelin Correspondence College. Seven years, Mr Styles! And at last I made it. Here it is. Standard Six Certificate, School Leaving, Third Class! I made it, Mr Styles. I made it. But I'm not finished. I'm going to take up for the Junior Certificate, then Matric . . . and you watch, Mr Styles. One day I walk out of my house, graduate, self-made! Bye-bye, Mr Styles,' . . . and he walked out of here happy man, self-made.

[*Back to his display-board; another photograph.*]

My best. Family Card. You know the Family Card? Good for business. Lot of people and they all want copies.

One Saturday morning. Suddenly a hell of a noise outside in the street. I thought: What's going on now? Next thing that door burst open and in they came! First the little ones, then the five- and six-year-olds. . . . I didn't know what was going on, man! Stupid children, coming to mess up my place. I was still trying to chse them out when the bigger boys and girls came through the door. Then it clicked. Family Card!

[*Changing his manner abruptly.*]

'Come in! Come in!'

[*Ushering a crowd of people into his studio.*]

. . . now the young men and women were coming in, then the mothers and fathers, uncles and aunties . . . the eldest son, a mature man, and finally . . .

[*Shaking his head with admiration at the memory.*]

the Old Man, the Grandfather! [*The 'old man' walks slowly and with dignity into the studio and sits down in the chair.*]

I looked at him. His grey hair was a sign of wisdom. His face, weather-beaten and lined with experience. Looking at it was like paging the volume of his history, written by himself. He was a living symbol of Life, of all it means and does to a man. I adored him. He sat there—half smiling, half serious—as if he had already seen the end of his road.

The eldest son said to me: 'Mr Styles, this is my father, my mother, my brothers and sisters, their wives and husbands, our children. Twenty-seven of us, Mr Styles. We have come to take a card. My father . . . ,' he pointed to the old man, '. . . my father always wanted it.'

I said: 'Certainly. Leave the rest to me.' I went to work.

[*Another graphic re-enactment of the scene as he describes it.*]

The old lady here, the eldest son there. Then the other one, with the other one. On this side I did something with the daughters, aunties, and one bachelor brother. Then in front of it all the eight-to-twelves, standing, in front of them the four-to-sevens, kneeling, and finally right on the floor everything that was left, sitting. Jesus, it was hard work, but finally I had them all sorted out and I went behind the camera.

[*Behind his camera.*]

Just starting to focus . . .

[*Imaginary child in front of the lens; Styles chases the child back to the family group.*]

'. . . Sit down! Sit down!'

Back to the camera, start to focus again. . . . Not One Of Them Was Smiling! I tried the old trick. 'Say cheese, please.' At first they just looked at me. 'Come on! Cheese!' The children were the first to pick it up.

[*Child's voice.*] 'Cheese. Cheese. Cheese.' Then the ones a little bit bigger—'Cheese'—then the next lot—'Cheese'—the uncles and aunties—'Cheese'—and finally the old man himself—'Cheese'! I thought the roof was going off, man! People outside in the street came and looked through the window. They joined in: 'Cheese.' When I looked again the mourners from the funeral parlour were there wiping away their tears and saying 'Cheese'. Pressed my little button and there it was—New Brighton's smile, twenty-seven variations. Don't you believe those bloody fools who make out we don't know how to smile!

Anyway, you should have seen me then. Moved the bachelor this side, sister-in-laws that side. Put the eldest son behind the old man. Reorganized the children. . . . [*Back behind his camera.*] 'Once again, please! Cheese!' Back to work . . . old man and old woman together, daughters behind them, sons on the side. Those that were kneeling now standing, those that were standing, now kneeling. . . . Ten times, friends! Each one different!

[*An exhausted Styles collapses in a chair.*]

When they walked out finally I almost said Never Again! A week later the eldest son came back for the cards. I had them ready. The moment he walked through that door I could see he was in trouble. He said to me: 'Mr Styles, we almost didn't make it. My father died two days after the card. He will never see it.' 'Come on,' I said. 'You're a man. One day or the other everyone of us must go home. Here. . . .' I grabbed the cards. 'Here. Look at your father and thank God for the time he was given on this earth.' We went through them together. He looked at them in silence. After the third one, the tear went slowly down his cheek.

But at the same time . . . I was watching him carefully . . . something started to happen as he saw his father there with himself, his brothers and sisters, and all the little grandchildren. He began to smile. 'That's it, brother,' I said. 'Smile! Smile at your father. Smile at the world.'

When he left, I thought of him going back to his little house somewhere in New Brighton, filled that day with the little mothers in black because a man had died. I saw my cards passing from hand to hand. I saw hands wipe away tears, and then the first timid little smiles.

You must understand one thing. We own nothing except ourselves. This world and its laws, allows us nothing, except ourselves. There is nothing we can leave behind when we die, except the memory of ourselves. I know what I'm talking about, friends—I had a father, and he died.

[*To the display-board.*]

Here he is. My father. That's him. Fought in the war. Second

World War. Fought at Tobruk. In Egypt. He fought in France so that this country and all the others could stay Free. When he came back they stripped him at the docks—his gun, his uniform, the dignity they'd allowed him for a few mad years because the world needed men to fight and be ready to sacrifice themselves for something called Freedom. In return they let him keep his scoff-tin and gave him a bicycle. Size twenty-eight. I remember, because it was too big for me. When he died, in a rotten old suitcase amongst some of his old rags, I found that photograph. That's all. That's all I have from him.

[*The display-board again.*]

Or this old lady. Mrs Matothlana. Used to stay in Sangocha Street. You remember! Her husband was arrested. . . .

[*Knock at the door.*]

Tell you about it later. Come in!

[A man *walks nervously into the studio. Dressed in an ill-fitting new double-breasted suit. He is carrying a plastic bag with a hat in it. His manner is hesitant and shy. Styles takes one look at him and breaks into an enormous smile.*]

[*An aside to the audience.*] A Dream!

[*To the man.*] Come in, my friend.

MAN. Mr Styles?

STYLES. That's me. Come in! You have come to take a card?

MAN. Snap.

STYLES. Yes, a card. Have you got a deposit?

MAN. Yes.

STYLES. Good. Let me just take your name down. You see, you pay deposit now, and when you come for the card, you pay the rest.

MAN. Yes.

STYLES [*to his desk and a black book for names and addresses*]. What is your name? [*The man hesitates, as if not sure of himself.*] Your name, please?

[*Pause.*]

Come on, my friend. You must surely have a name.

MAN [*pulling himself together, but still very nervous*]. Robert Zwelinzima.

STYLES [*writing*]. 'Robert Zwelinzima.' Address?

MAN [*swallowing*]. Fifty, Mapija Street.

STYLES [*writes, then pauses*]. 'Fifty, Mapija?'

MAN. Yes.

STYLES. You staying with Buntu?

MAN. Buntu.

STYLES. Very good somebody that one. Came here for his Wedding Card. Always helping people. If that man was white they'd call him a liberal.

[*Now finished writing. Back to his customer.*]

All right. How many cards do you want?

MAN. One card.

STYLES [*disappointed*]. Only one?

MAN. One.

STYLES. How do you want to take the card?

[*The man is not sure of what the question means.*]

You can take the card standing . . .

[*Styles strikes a stylish pose next to the table.*]

sitting . . .

[*Another pose . . . this time in the chair.*]

anyhow. How do you want it?

MAN. Anyhow.

STYLES. Right. Sit down.

[*Robert hesitates.*]

Sit down!

[*Styles fetches a vase with plastic flowers, dusts them off, and places them on the table. Robert holds up his plastic bag.*]

What you got there?

[*Out comes the hat.*]

Aha! Stetson. Put it on, my friend.

[*Robert handles it shyly.*]

You can put it on, Robert.

[*Robert pulls it on. Styles does up one of his jacket buttons.*]

18

Winston Ntshona as Sizwe Bansi.

What a beautiful suit, my friend! Where did you buy it?

MAN. Sales House.

STYLES [*quoting a sales slogan*]. 'Where the Black world buys the best. Six months to pay. Pay as you wear.'

[*Nudges Robert.*]

. . . and they never repossess!

[*They share a laugh.*]

What are you going to do with this card?

[*Chatting away as he goes to his camera and sets it up for the photo. Robert watches the preparations apprehensively.*]

MAN. Send it to my wife.

STYLES. Your wife!

MAN. Nowetu.

STYLES. Where's your wife?

MAN. King William's Town.

STYLES [*exaggerated admiration*]. At last! The kind of man I like. Not one of those foolish young boys who come here to find work and then forget their families back home. A man, with responsibility!
Where do you work?

MAN. Feltex.

STYLES. I hear they pay good there.

MAN. Not bad.

[*He is now very tense, staring fixedly at the camera. Styles straightens up behind it.*]

STYLES. Come on, Robert! You want your wife to get a card with her husband looking like he's got all the worries in the world on his back? What will she think? 'My poor husband is in trouble!' You must smile!

[*Robert shamefacedly relaxes a little and starts to smile.*]

That's it!

[*He relaxes still more. Beginning to enjoy himself. Uncertainly produces a very fancy pipe from one of his pockets.
Styles now really warming to the assignment.*]

Look, have you ever walked down the passage to the office with the big glass door and the board outside: 'Manager—

Bestuurder'. Imagine it, man, you, Robert Zwelinzima, behind a desk in an office like that! It can happen, Robert. Quick promotion to Chief Messenger. I'll show you what we do.

[*Styles produces a Philips' class-room map of the world, which he hangs behind the table as a backdrop to the photo.*]

Look at it, Robert. America, England, Africa, Russia, Asia!

[*Carried away still further by his excitement, Styles finds a cigarette, lights it, and gives it to Robert to hold. The latter is now ready for the 'card' . . . pipe in one hand and cigarette in the other. Styles stands behind his camera and admires his handiwork.*]

Mr Robert Zwelinzima, Chief Messenger at Feltex, sitting in his office with the world behind him. Smile, Robert. Smile!

[*Studying his subject through the viewfinder of the camera.*]

Lower your hand, Robert . . . towards the ashtray . . . more . . . now make a four with your legs. . . .

[*He demonstrates behind the camera. Robert crosses his legs.*]

Hold it, Robert. . . . Keep on smiling . . . that's it. . . . [*presses the release button—the shutter clicks.*]

Beautiful! All right, Robert.

[*Robert and his smile remain frozen.*]

Robert. You can relax now. It's finished!

MAN. Finished?

STYLES. Yes. You just want the one card?

MAN. Yes.

STYLES. What happens if you lose it? Hey? I've heard stories about those postmen, Robert. *Yo!* Sit on the side of the road and open the letters they should be delivering! 'Dear wife . . .' —one rand this side, letter thrown away. 'Dear wife . . .'— another rand this side, letter thrown away. You want that to happen to you? Come on! What about a movie, man?

MAN. Movie?

STYLES. Don't you know the movie?

MAN. No.

STYLES. Simple! You just walk you see . . .

[*Styles demonstrates; at a certain point freezes in mid-stride.*]

. . . and I take the card! Then you can write to your wife:

John Kani and Winston Ntshona.

'Dear wife, I am coming home at Christmas. . . .' Put the card in your letter and post it. Your wife ópens the letter and what does she see? Her Robert, walking home to her! She shows it to the children. 'Look, children, your daddy is coming!' The children jump and clap their hands: 'Daddy is coming! Daddy is coming!'

MAN [*excited by the picture Styles has conjured up*]. All right!

STYLES. You want a movie?

MAN. I want a movie.

STYLES. That's my man! Look at this, Robert.

[*Styles reverses the map hanging behind the table to reveal a gaudy painting of a futuristic city.*]

City of the Future! Look at it. Mr Robert Zwelinzima, man about town, future head of Feltex, walking through the City of the Future!

MAN [*examining the backdrop with admiration. He recognizes a landmark*]. OK.

STYLES. OK Bazaars . . . [*the other buildings*] . . . Mutual Building Society, Barclays Bank . . . the lot!
What you looking for, Robert?

MAN. Feltex.

STYLES. Yes . . . well, you see, I couldn't fit everything on, Robert. But if I had had enough space Feltex would have been here.

[*To his table for props.*]

Walking-stick . . . newspaper. . . .

MAN [*diffidently*]. I don't read.

STYLES. That is not important, my friend. You think all those monkeys carrying newspapers can read? They look at the pictures.

[*After 'dressing' Robert with the props he moves back to his camera.*]

This is going to be beautiful, Robert. My best card. I must send one to the magazines.
All right, Robert, now move back. Remember what I showed you. Just walk towards me and right in front of the City of the Future. I'll take the picture. Ready? Now come, Robert. . . .

[*Pipe in mouth, walking-stick in hand, newspaper under the other arm, Robert takes a jaunty step and then freezes, as Styles had shown him earlier.*]

Come, Robert. . . .

[*Another step.*]

Just one more, Robert. . . .

[*Another step.*]

Stop! Hold it, Robert. Hold it!

[*The camera flash goes off; simultaneously a blackout except for one light on Robert, frozen in the pose that will appear in the picture. We are in fact looking at the photograph. It 'comes to life'· and dictates the letter that will accompany it to Nowetu in King William's Town.*]

MAN. Nowetu . . .

[*Correcting himself.*]

Dear Nowetu,

I've got wonderful news for you in this letter. My troubles are over, I think. You won't believe it, but I must tell you. Sizwe Bansi, in a manner of speaking, is dead! I'll tell you what I can.

As you know, when I left the Railway Compound I went to stay with a friend of mine called Zola. A very good friend that, Nowetu. In fact he was even trying to help me find some job. But that's not easy, Nowetu, because Port Elizabeth is a big place, a very big place with lots of factories but also lots of people looking for a job like me. There are so many men, Nowetu, who have left their places because they are dry and have come here to find work!

After a week with Zola, I was in big trouble. The headman came around, and after a lot of happenings which I will tell you when I see you, they put a stamp in my passbook which said I must leave Port Elizabeth at once in three days time. I was very much unhappy, Nowetu. I couldn't stay with Zola because if the headman found me there again my troubles would be even bigger. So Zola took me to a friend of his called Buntu, and asked him if I could stay with him until I decided what to do. . . .

[*Buntu's house in New Brighton. Table and two chairs. Robert, in a direct continuation of the preceding scene, is already there, as Buntu,*] *jacket slung over his shoulder, walks in. Holds out his hand to Robert.*]

BUNTU. Hi. Buntu.

[*They shake hands.*]

MAN. Sizwe Bansi.

BUNTU. Sit down.

[*They sit.*]

Zola told me you were coming. Didn't have time to explain anything. Just asked if you could spend a few nights here. You can perch yourself on that sofa in the corner. I'm alone at the moment. My wife is a domestic . . . sleep-in at Kabega Park . . . only comes home weekends. Hot today, hey?

[*In the course of this scene Buntu will busy himself first by having a wash—basin and jug of water on the table—and then by changing from his working clothes preparatory to going out. Sizwe Bansi stays in his chair.*]

What's your problem, friend?

MAN. I've got no permit to stay in Port Elizabeth.

BUNTU. Where do you have a permit to stay?

MAN. King William's Town.

BUNTU. How did they find out?

MAN [*tells his story with the hesitation and uncertainty of the illiterate. When words fail him he tries to use his hands.*]

I was staying with Zola, as you know. I was very happy there. But one night . . . I was sleeping on the floor . . . I heard some noises and when I looked up I saw torches shining in through the window . . . then there was a loud knocking on the door. When I got up Zola was there in the dark . . . he was trying to whisper something. I think he was saying I must hide. So I crawled under the table. The headman came in and looked around and found me hiding under the table . . . and dragged me out.

BUNTU. Raid?

MAN. Yes, it was a raid. I was just wearing my pants. My shirt was lying on the other side. I just managed to grab it as they were pushing me out. . . . I finished dressing in the van. They drove straight to the administration office . . . and then

23

from there they drove to the Labour Bureau. I was made to stand in the passage there, with everybody looking at me and shaking their heads like they knew I was in big trouble. Later I was taken into an office and made to stand next to the door. . . . The white man behind the desk had my book and he also looked at me and shook his head. Just then one other white man came in with a card. . . .

BUNTU. A card?

MAN. He was carrying a card.

BUNTU. Pink card?

MAN. Yes, the card was pink.

BUNTU. Record card. Your whole bloody life is written down on that. Go on.

MAN. Then the first white man started writing something on the card . . . and just then somebody came in carrying a. . . .

[*demonstrates what he means by banging a clenched fist on the table.*]

BUNTU. A stamp?

MAN. Yes, a stamp. [*Repeats the action.*] He was carrying a stamp.

BUNTU. And then?

MAN. He put it on my passbook.

BUNTU. Let me see your book?

[*Sizwe produces his passbook from the back-pocket of his trousers. Buntu examines it.*]

Shit! You know what this is? [*The stamp.*]

MAN. I can't read.

BUNTU. Listen . . . [*reads*]. 'You are required to report to the Bantu Affairs Commissioner, King William's Town, within three days of the above-mentioned date for the. . . .' You should have been home yesterday! . . . 'for the purpose of repatriation to home district.' Influx Control.
You're in trouble, Sizwe.

MAN. I don't want to leave Port Elizabeth.

BUNTU. Maybe. But if that book says go, you go.

MAN. Can't I maybe burn this book and get a new one?

BANTU. Burn that book? Stop kidding yourself, Sizwe! Anyway

24

suppose you do. You must immediately go apply for a new one. Right? And until that new one comes, be careful the police don't stop you and ask for your book. Into the Court-room, brother. Charge: Failing to produce Reference Book on Demand. Five rand or five days. Finally the new book comes. Down to the Labour Bureau for a stamp . . . it's got to be endorsed with permission to be in this area. White man at the Labour Bureau takes the book, looks at it—doesn't look at you!—goes to the big machine and feeds in your number . . .

[*Buntu goes through the motions of punching out a number on a computer.*]

. . . card jumps out, he reads: 'Sizwe Bansi. Endorsed to King William's Town. . . .' Takes your book, fetches that same stamp, and in it goes again. So you burn that book, or throw it away, and get another one. Same thing happens.

[*Buntu feeds the computer; the card jumps out.*]

'Sizwe Bansi. Endorsed to King William's Town. . . .' Stamp goes in the third time. . . . But this time it's also into a van and off to the Native Commissioner's Office; card around your neck with your number on it; escort on both sides and back to King William's Town. They make you pay for the train fare too!

MAN. I think I will try to look for some jobs in the garden.

BUNTU. You? Job as a garden-boy? Don't you read the newspapers?

MAN. I can't read.

BUNTU. I'll tell you what the little white ladies say: 'Domestic vacancies. I want a garden-boy with good manners and a wide knowledge of seasons and flowers. Book in order.' Yours in order? Anyway what the hell do you know about seasons and flowers? [*After a moment's thought.*] Do you know any white man who's prepared to give you a job?

MAN. No. I don't know any white man.

BUNTU. Pity. We might have been able to work something then. You talk to the white man, you see, and ask him to write a letter saying he's got a job for you. You take that letter from the white man and go back to King William's Town, where you show it to the Native Commissioner there. The Native Commissioner in King William's Town reads that letter

25

from the white man in Port Elizabeth who is ready to give you
the job. He then writes a letter back to the Native Commissioner in Port Elizabeth. So you come back here with the
two letters. Then the Native Commissioner in Port Elizabeth
reads the letter from the Native Commissioner in King
William's Town together with the first letter from the white
man who is prepared to give you a job, and he says when he reads
the letters: Ah yes, this man Sizwe Bansi can get a job. So the
Native Commissioner in Port Elizabeth then writes a letter
which you take with the letters from the Native Commissioner
in King William's Town and the white man in Port Elizabeth,
to the Senior Officer at the Labour Bureau, who reads all the
letters. Then he will put the right stamp in your book and
give you another letter from himself which together with the
letters from the white man and the two Native Affairs
Commissioners, you take to the Administration Office here in
New Brighton and make an application for Residence Permit,
so that you don't fall victim of raids again. Simple.

MAN. Maybe I can start a little business selling potatoes and. . . .

BUNTU. Where do you get the potatoes and . . .?

MAN. I'll buy them.

BUNTU. With what?

MAN. Borrow some money. . . .

BUNTU. Who is going to lend money to a somebody endorsed
to hell and gone out in the bush? And how you going to
buy your potatoes at the market without a Hawker's Licence?
Same story, Sizwe. You won't get that because of the bloody
stamp in your book.
There's no way out, Sizwe. You're not the first one who has
tried to find it. Take my advice and catch that train back to
King William's Town. If you need work so bad go knock on
the door of the Mines Recruiting Office. Dig gold for the white
man. That's the only time they don't worry about Influx
Control.

MAN. I don't want to work on the mines. There is no money
there. And it's dangerous, under the ground. Many black men
get killed when the rocks fall. You can die there.

BUNTU [stopped by the last remark into taking possibly his first real
look at Sizwe].

26

You don't want to die.

MAN. I don't want to die.

BUNTU [*stops whatever he is doing to sit down and talk to Sizwe with an intimacy that was not there before.*]
You married, Sizwe?

MAN. Yes.

BUNTU. How many children?

MAN. I've got four children.

BUNTU. Boys? Girls?

MAN. I've got three boys and one girl.

BUNTU. Schooling?

MAN. Two are schooling. The other two stay at home with their mother.

BUNTU. Your wife is not working.

MAN. The place where we stay is fifteen miles from town. There is only one shop there. Baas van Wyk. He has already got a woman working for him. King William's Town is a dry place Mr Buntu . . . very small and too many people. That is why I don't want to go back.

BUNTU. *Ag*, friend . . . I don't know! I'm also married. One child.

MAN. Only one?

BUNTU. *Ja*, my wife attends this Birth Control Clinic rubbish. The child is staying with my mother.
[*Shaking his head.*] *Hai*, Sizwe! If I had to tell you the trouble I had before I could get the right stamps in my book, even though I was born in this area! The trouble I had before I could get a decent job . . . born in this area! The trouble I had to get this two-roomed house . . . born in this area!

MAN. Why is there so much trouble, Mr Buntu?

BUNTU. Two weeks back I went to a funeral with a friend of mine. Out in the country. An old relative of his passed away. Usual thing . . . sermons in the house, sermons in the church, sermons at the graveside. I thought they were never going to stop talking! At the graveside service there was one fellow, a lay preacher . . . short man, neat little moustache, wearing one of those old-fashioned double-breasted black suits. . . . *Haai!* He was wonderful. While he talked he had a gesture with his hands . . . like this . . . that reminded me of our youth, when we learnt to fight with kieries. His text was 'Going Home'. He handled it well, Sizwe. Started by saying that the first man to sign the Death Contract with God, was Adam, when he sinned in Eden. Since that day, wherever Man is, or whatever he does, he is never without his faithful companion, Death. So with Outa Jacob . . . the dead man's name . . . he has at last accepted the terms of his contract with God.

But in his life, friends, he walked the roads of this land. He helped print those footpaths which lead through the bush and over the veld . . . footpaths which his children are now walking. He worked on farms from this district down to the coast and north as far as Pretoria. I knew him. He was a friend. Many people knew Outa Jacob. For a long time he worked for Baas van der Walt. But when the old man died his young son Hendrik said: 'I don't like you. Go!' Outa Jacob picked up his load and put it on his shoulders. His wife followed. He went to the next farm . . . through the fence, up to the house . . . : 'Work, please, Baas.' Baas Potgieter took him. He stayed a long time there too, until one day there was trouble between the Madam and his wife. Jacob and his wife were walking again. The load on his back was heavier, he wasn't so young any more, and there were children behind them now as well. On to the next farm. No work. The next one. No work. Then the next one. A little time there. But the drought was bad and the farmer said: 'Sorry, Jacob. The cattle are dying. I'm moving to the city.' Jacob picked up his load yet again. So it went, friends. On and on . . . until he arrived there. [*The grave at his feet.*] Now at last it's over. No matter how hard-arsed the boer on this farm wants to be, he cannot move Outa Jacob. He has reached Home.

[*Pause.*]

That's it, brother. The only time we'll find peace is when they dig a hole for us and press our face into the earth.

[*Putting on his coat.*]

Ag, to hell with it. If we go on like this much longer we'll do the digging for them.

[*Changing his tone.*]

You know Sky's place, Sizwe?

MAN. No.

BUNTU. Come. Let me give you a treat. I'll do you there.

[*Exit Buntu.*
Blackout except for a light on Sizwe. He continues his letter to Nowetu.]

MAN. Sky's place? [*Shakes his head and laughs.*] Hey, Nowetu! When I mention that name again, I get a headache ... the same headache I had when I woke up in Buntu's place the next morning. You won't believe what it was like. You cannot! It would be like you walking down Pickering Street in King William's Town and going into Koekemoer's Café to buy bread, and what do you see sitting there at the smart table and chairs? Your husband, Sizwe Bansi, being served ice-cream and cool drinks by old Mrs Koekemoer herself. Such would be your surprise if you had seen me at Sky's place. Only they weren't serving cool drinks and ice-cream. No! First-class booze, Nowetu. And it wasn't old Mrs Koekemoer serving me, but a certain lovely and beautiful lady called Miss Nkonyemi. And it wasn't just your husband Sizwe sitting there with all the most important people of New Brighton, but *Mister* Bansi.

[*He starts to laugh.*]

Mister Bansi!

[*As the laugh gets bigger, Sizwe rises to his feet.*]

[*The street outside Sky's Shebeen in New Brighton. Our man is amiably drunk. He addresses the audience.*]

MAN. Do you know who I am, friend? Take my hand, friend. Take my hand. I am Mister Bansi, friend. Do you know where I come from? I come from Sky's place, friend. A most wonderful place. I met everybody there, good people. I've been drinking, my friends—brandy, wine, beer. ... Don't you want to go in there, good people? Let's all go to Sky's place. [*Shouting.*] Mr Buntu! Mr Buntu!

[*Buntu enters shouting goodbye to friends at the Shebeen. He joins Sizwe. Buntu, though not drunk, is also amiably talkative under the influence of a good few drinks.*]

BUNTU [*discovering the audience*]. Hey, where did you get all these wonderful people?

MAN. I just found them here, Mr Buntu.

BUNTU. Wonderful!

MAN. I'm inviting them to Sky's place, Mr Buntu.

BUNTU. You tell them about Sky's?

MAN. I told them about Sky's place, Mr Buntu.

BUNTU [*to the audience*]. We been having a time there, man!

MAN. They know it. I told them everything.

BUNTU [*laughing*]. Sizwe! We had our fun there.

MAN. Hey ... hey....

BUNTU. Remember that Member of the Advisory Board?

MAN. Hey. ... Hey ... Mr Buntu! You know I respect you, friend. You must call me nice.

BUNTU. What do you mean?

MAN [*clumsy dignity*]. I'm not just Sizwe no more. He might have walked in, but Mr Bansi walked out!

BUNTU [*playing along*]. I am terribly sorry, Mr Bansi. I apologize for my familiarity. Please don't be offended.

[*Handing over one of the two oranges he is carrying.*]

Allow me ... with the compliments of Miss Nkonyeni.

MAN [*taking the orange with a broad but sheepish grin*]. Miss Nkonyeni!

BUNTU. Sweet dreams, Mr Bansi.

MAN [*tears the orange with his thumbs and starts eating it messily*]. Lovely lady, Mr Buntu.

BUNTU [*leaves Sizwe with a laugh. To the audience*]. Back there in the Shebeen a Member of the Advisory Board hears that he comes from King William's Town. He goes up to Sizwe. 'Tell me, Mr Bansi, what do you think of Ciskeian Independence?'

MAN [*interrupting*]. Ja, I remember that one. Bloody Mister Member of the Advisory Board. Talking about Ciskeian Independence!

[*To the audience.*]

I must tell you, friend ... when a car passes or the wind blows

up the dust, Ciskeian Independence makes you cough. I'm
telling you, friend . . . put a man in a pondok and call that
Independence? My good friend, let me tell you . . . Ciskeian
Independence is shit!

BUNTU Or that other chap! Old Jolobe. The fat tycoon man!
[to the audience] Comes to me . . . [pompous voice] . . . 'Your friend,
Mr Bansi, is he on an official visit to town?' 'No,' I said,
'Mr Bansi is on an official walkout!' [Buntu thinks this is a big
joke.]

MAN [stubbornly]. I'm here to stay.

BUNTU [looking at his watch]. Hey, Sizwe. . . .

MAN [reproachfully]. Mr Buntu!

BUNTU [correcting himself]. Mr Bansi, it is getting late. I've
got to work tomorrow. Care to lead the way, Mr Bansi?

MAN. You think I can't? You think Mr Bansi is lost?

BUNTU. I didn't say that.

MAN. You are thinking it, friend. I'll show you. This is Chinga
Street.

BUNTU. Very good! But which way do we . . . ?

MAN [setting off]. This way.

BUNTU [pulling him back]. Mistake. You're heading for Site
and Service and a lot of trouble with the Tsotsis.

MAN [the opposite direction]. That way.

BUNTU. Lead on. I'm right behind you.

MAN. Ja, you are right, Mr Buntu. There is Newell High
School. Now. . . .

BUNTU. Think carefully!

MAN. . . . when we were going to Sky's we had Newell in front.
So when we leave Sky's we put Newell behind.

BUNTU. Very good!

[An appropriate change in direction. They continue walking, and
eventually arrive at a square, with roads leading off in many directions.
Sizwe is lost. He wanders around, uncertain of the direction to
take.]

MAN. Haai, Mr Buntu . . . !

BUNTU. Mbizweni Square.

31

MAN. *Yo!* Cross-roads to hell, wait . . . [*Closer look at landmark.*] . . . that building . . . Rio Cinema! So we must. . . .

BUNTU. Rio Cinema? With a white cross on top, bell outside, and the big show on Sundays?

MAN [*sheepishly*]. You're right, friend. I've got it, Mr Buntu. That way.

[*He starts off. Buntu watches him.*]

BUNTU. Goodbye. King William's Town a hundred and fifty miles. Don't forget to write.

MAN [*hurried about-turn*]. Haai . . . haai. . . .

BUNTU. Okay, Sizwe, I'll take over from here. But just hang on for a second I want to have a piss. Don't move!

[*Buntu disappears into the dark.*]

MAN. *Haai,* Sizwe! You are a country fool! Leading Mr Buntu and Mr Bansi astray. You think you know this place New Brighton? You know nothing!

[*Buntu comes running back.*]

BUNTU [*urgently*]. Let's get out of here.

MAN. Wait, Mr Buntu, I'm telling that fool Sizwe. . . .

BUNTU. Come on! There's trouble there . . . [*pointing in the direction from which he has come*] . . . let's move.

MAN. Wait, Mr Buntu, wait. Let me first tell that Sizwe. . . .

BUNTU. There's a dead man lying there!

MAN. Dead man?

BUNTU. I thought I was just pissing on a pile of rubbish, but when I looked carefully I saw it was a man. Dead. Covered in blood. Tsotsis must have got him. Let's get the hell out of here before anybody sees us.

MAN. Buntu . . . Buntu. . . .

BUNTU. Listen to me, Sizwe! The Tsotsis might still be around.

MAN. Buntu. . . .

BUNTU. Do you want to join him?

MAN. I don't want to join him.

BUNTU. Then come.

MAN. Wait, Buntu.

BUNTU. Jesus! If Zola had told me how much trouble you were going to be!

MAN. Buntu, ... we must report that man to the police station.

BUNTU. Police Station! Are you mad? You drunk, passbook not in order ... 'We've come to report a dead man, Sergeant.' 'Grab them!' Case closed. We killed him.

MAN. Mr Buntu, ... we can't leave him. ...

BUNTU. Please, Sizwe!

MAN. Wait. Let's carry him home.

BUNTU. Jst like that! Walk through New Brighton streets, at this hour, carrying a dead man. Anyway we don't know where he stays. Come.

MAN. Wait, Buntu, ... listen. ...

BUNTU. Sizwe!

MAN. Buntu, we can know where he stays. That passbook of his will talk. It talks, friend, like mine. His passbook will tell you.

BUNTU [*after a moment's desperate hesitation*]. You really want to land me in the shit, hey.
  Disappears into the dark again.]

MAN. It will tell you in good English where he stays. My passbook talks good English too ... big words that Sizwe can't read and doesn't understand. Sizwe wants to stay here in New Brighton and find a job; passbook says, 'No! Report back.'
Sizwe wants to feed his wife and children; passbook says, 'No. Endorsed out.'
Sizwe wants to. ...
  [*Buntu reappears, a passbook in his hand. Looks around furtively and moves to the light under a lamp-post.*]
They never told us it would be like that when they introduced it. They said: Book of Life! Your friend! You'll never get lost! They told us lies.
  [*He joins Buntu who is examining the book.*]

BUNTU. *Haai!* Look at him [*the photograph in the book, reading*]. 'Robert Zwelinzima. Tribe: Xhosa. Native Identification Number. ...'

MAN. Where does he stay, Buntu?

33

BUNTU [*paging through the book*]. Worked at Dorman Long seven years . . . Kilomet Engineering . . . eighteen months . . . Anderson Hardware two years . . . now unemployed. Hey, look, Sizwe! He's one up on you. He's got a work-seeker's permit.

MAN. Where does he stay, Buntu?

BUNTU. Lodger's Permit at 42 Mdala Street. From there to Sangocha Street . . . now at. . . .

[*Pause. Closes the book abruptly.*]

To hell with it I'm not going *there*.

MAN. Where, Buntu?

BUNTU [*emphatically*]. I Am Not Going There!

MAN. Buntu. . . .

BUNTU. You know where he is staying now? Single Men's Quarters! If you think I'm going there this time of the night you got another guess coming.

[*Sizwe doesn't understand.*]

Look, Sizwe . . . I stay in a house, there's a street name and a number. Easy to find. Ask anybody . . . Mapija Street? That way. You know what Single Men's Quarters is? Big bloody concentration camp with rows of things that look like train carriages. Six doors to each! Twelve people behind each door! You want me to go there now? Knock on the first one: 'Does Robert Zwelinzima live here?' 'No!' Next one: 'Does Robert . . . ?' 'Bugger off, we're trying to sleep!' Next one: 'Does Robert Zwelinzima . . . ?' They'll fuck us up, man! I'm putting this book back and we're going home.

MAN. Buntu!

BUNTU [*half-way back to the alleyway*]. What?

MAN. Would you do that to me, friend? If the Tsotsis had stabbed Sizwe, and left him lying there, would you walk away from him as well?

[*The accusation stops Buntu.*]

Would you leave me lying there, wet with your piss? I wish I was dead. I wish I was dead because I don't care a damn about anything any more.

[*Turning away from Buntu to the audience.*]

What's happening in this world, good people? Who cares for who in this world? Who wants who?

Who wants me, friend? What's wrong with me? I'm a man. I've got eyes to see. I've got ears to listen when people talk. I've got a head to think good things. What's wrong with me?

[*Starts to tear off his clothes.*]

Look at me! I'm a man. I've got legs. I can run with a wheelbarrow full of cement! I'm strong! I'm a man. Look! I've got a wife. I've got four children. How many has he made, lady? [*The man sitting next to her.*] Is he a man? What has he got that I haven't . . . ?

[*A thoughtful Buntu rejoins them, the dead man's reference book still in his hand.*]

BUNTU. Let me see your book?

[*Sizwe doesn't respond.*]

Give me your book!

MAN. Are you a policeman now, Buntu?

BUNTU. Give me your bloody book, Sizwe!

MAN [*handing it over*]. Take it, Buntu. Take this book and read it carefully, friend, and tell me what it says about me. Buntu, does that book tell you I'm a man?

[*Buntu studies the two books. Sizwe turns back to the audience.*]

That bloody book . . . ! People, do you know? No! Wherever you go . . . it's that bloody book. You go to school, it goes too. Go to work, it goes too. Go to church and pray and sing lovely hymns, it sits there with you. Go to hospital to die, it lies there too!

[*Buntu has collected Sizwe's discarded clothing.*]

BUNTU. Come!

[*Buntu's house, as earlier. Table and two chairs. Buntu pushes Sizwe down into a chair. Sizwe still muttering, starts to struggle back into his clothes. Buntu opens the two reference books and places them side by side on the table. He produces a pot of glue, then very carefully tears out the photograph in each book. A dab of glue on the back of each and then Sizwe's goes back into Robert's book, and Robert's into Sizwe's. Sizwe watches this operation, at first uninterestedly, but when he realizes what Buntu is up to, with growing*]

35

alarm. When he is finished, Buntu pushes the two books in front of Sizwe.]

MAN [*shaking his head emphatically*]. *Yo! Haai, haai.* No, Buntu.

BUNTU. It's a chance.

MAN. *Haai, haai, haai . . .*

BUNTU. It's your only chance!

MAN. No, Buntu! What's it mean? That me, Sizwe Bansi. . . .

BUNTU. Is dead.

MAN. I'm not dead, friend.

BUNTU. We burn this book . . . [*Sizwe's original*] . . . and Sizwe Bansi disappears off the face of the earth.

MAN. What about the man we left lying in the alleyway?

BUNTU. Tomorrow the Flying Squad passes there and finds him. Check in his pockets . . . no passbook. Mount Road Mortuary. After three days nobody has identified him. Pauper's Burial. Case closed.

MAN. And then?

BUNTU. Tomorrow I contact my friend Norman at Feltex. He's a boss-boy there. I tell him about another friend, Robert Zwelinzima, book in order, who's looking for a job. You roll up later, hand over the book to the white man. Who does Robert Zwelinzima look like? You! Who gets the pay on Friday? You, man!

MAN. What about all that shit at the Labour Bureau, Buntu?

BUNTU. You don't have to there. This chap had a work-seeker's permit, Sizwe. All you do is hand over the book to the white man. *He* checks at the Labour Bureau. They check with their big machine. 'Robert Zwelinzima has the right to be employed and stay in this town.'

MAN. I don't want to lose my name, Buntu.

BUNTU. You mean you don't want to lose your bloody passbook! You love it, hey?

MAN. Buntu. I cannot lose my name.

BUNTU [*leaving the table*]. All right, I was only trying to help. As Robert Zwelinzima you could have stayed and worked in this town. As Sizwe Bansi . . . ? Start walking, friend. King William's Town. Hundred and fifty miles. And don't waste any time!

You've got to be there by yesterday. Hope you enjoy it.

MAN. Buntu. . . .

BUNTU. Lots of scenery in a hundred and fifty miles.

MAN. Buntu! . . .

BUNTU. Maybe a better idea is just to wait until they pick you up. Save yourself all that walking. Into the train with the escort! Smart stuff, hey. Hope it's not too crowded though. Hell of a lot of people being kicked out, I hear.

MAN. Buntu! . . .

BUNTU. But once you're back! Sit down on the side of the road next to your pondok with your family . . . the whole Bansi clan on leave . . . for life! Hey, that sounds okay. Watching all the cars passing, and as you say, friend, cough your bloody lungs out with Ciskeian Independence.

MAN [*now really desperate*]. Buntu!!!

BUNTU. What you waiting for? Go!

MAN. Buntu.

BUNTU. What?

MAN. What about my wife, Nowetu?

BUNTU. What about her?

MAN [*maudlin tears*]. Her loving husband, Siwze Bansi, is dead!

BUNTU. So what! She's going to marry a better man.

MAN [*bridling*]. Who?

BUNTU. You . . . Robert Zwelinzima.

MAN [*thoroughly confused*]. How can I marry my wife, Buntu?

BUNTU. Get her down here and I'll introduce you.

MAN. Don't make jokes, Buntu. Robert . . . Sizwe . . . I'm all mixed up. Who am I?

BUNTU. A fool who is not taking his chance.

MAN. And my children! Their father is Sizwe Bansi. They're registered at school under Bansi. . . .

BUNTU. Are you really worried about your children, friend, or are you just worried about yourself and your bloody name? Wake up, man! Use that book and with your pay on Friday you'll have a real chance to do something for them.

37

MAN. I'm afraid. How do I get used to Robert? How do I live as another man's ghost?

BUNTU. Wasn't Sizwe Bansi a ghost?

MAN. No!

BUNTU. No? When the white man looked at you at the Labour Bureau what did he see? A man with dignity or a bloody passbook with an N.I. number? Isn't that a ghost? When the white man sees you walk down the street and calls out, 'Hey, John! Come here' . . . to you, *Sizwe Bansi* . . . isn't that a ghost? Or when his little child calls you 'Boy' . . . you a man, circumcised with a wife and four children . . . isn't that a ghost? Stop fooling yourself. All I'm saying is be a real ghost, if that is what they want, what they've turned us into. Spook them into hell, man!

[*Sizwe is silenced. Buntu realizes his words are beginning to reach the other man. He paces quietly, looking for his next move. He finds it.*]

Suppose you try my plan. Friday. Roughcasting section at Feltex. Paytime. Line of men—non-skilled labourers. White man with the big box full of pay-packets.

'John Kani!' 'Yes, sir!' Pay-packet is handed over. 'Thank you, sir.'

Another one. [*Buntu reads the name on an imaginary pay-packet.*] 'Winston Ntshona!' 'Yes, sir!' Pay-packet over. 'Thank you, sir!' Another one. 'Fats Bhokolane!' '*Hier is ek, my baas!*' Pay-packet over. '*Dankie, my baas!*'

Another one. 'Robert Zwelinzima!'

[*No response from Sizwe.*]

'Robert Zwelinzima!'

MAN. Yes, sir.

BUNTU [*handing him the imaginary pay-packet*]. Open it. Go on.

[*Takes back the packet, tears it open, empties its contents on the table, and counts it.*]

Five . . . ten . . . eleven . . . twelve . . . and ninety-nine cents. In *your* pocket!

[*Buntu again paces quietly, leaving Sizwe to think. Eventually. . . .*]

Saturday. Man in overalls, twelve rand ninety-nine cents

in the back pocket, walking down Main Street looking for Sales House. Finds it and walks in. Salesman comes forward to meet him.

'I've come to buy a suit.' Salesman is very friendly.

'Certainly. Won't you take a seat. I'll get the forms. I'm sure you want to open an account, sir. Six months to pay. But first I'll need all your particulars.'

[*Buntu has turned the table, with Sizwe on the other side, into the imaginary scene at Sales House.*]

BUNTU [*pencil poised, ready to fill in a form*]. Your name, please, sir?

MAN [*playing along uncertainly*]. Robert Zwelinzima.

BUNTU [*writing*]. 'Robert Zwelinzima.' Address?

MAN. Fifty, Mapija Street.

BUNTU. Where do you work?

MAN. Feltex.

BUNTU. And how much do you get paid?

MAN. Twelve . . . twelve rand ninety-nine cents.

BUNTU. N.I. Number, please?

[*Sizwe hesitates.*]

Your Native Identity number please?

[*Sizwe is still uncertain. Buntu abandons the act and picks up Robert Zwelinzima's passbook. He reads out the number.*]

N—I—3—8—1—1—8—6—3.

Burn that into your head, friend. You hear me? It's more important than your name.

N.I. number . . . three. . . .

MAN. Three.

BUNTU. Eight.

MAN. Eight.

BUNTU. One.

MAN. One.

BUNTU. One.

MAN. One.

BUNTU. Eight.

MAN. Eight.

BUNTU. Six.

MAN. Six.

BUNTU. Three.

MAN. Three.

BUNTU. Again. Three.

MAN. Three.

BUNTU. Eight.

MAN. Eight.

BUNTU. One.

MAN. One.

BUNTU. One.

MAN. One.

BUNTU. Eight.

MAN. Eight.

BUNTU. Six.

MAN. Six.

BUNTU. Three.

MAN. Three.

BUNTU [*picking up his pencil and returning to the role of the salesman*]. N.I. number, please.

MAN [*pausing frequently, using his hands to remember*]. Three . . . eight . . . one . . . one . . . eight . . . six . . . three. . . .

BUNTU [*abandoning the act*]. Good boy.

[*He paces. Sizwe sits and waits.*]

Sunday. Man in a Sales House suit, hat on top, going to church. Hymn book and bible under the arm. Sits down in the front pew. Priest in the pulpit.

[*Buntu jumps on to a chair in his new role. Sizwe kneels.*]

The Time has come!

MAN. Amen!

BUNTU. Pray, brothers and sisters. . . . Pray. . . . Now!

MAN. Amen.

BUNTU. The Lord wants to save you. Hand yourself over to

him, while there is still time, while Jesus is still prepared to listen to you.

MAN [*carried away by what he is feeling*]. Amen, Jesus!

BUNTU. Be careful, my brothers and sisters. . . .

MAN. Hallelujah!

BUNTU. Be careful lest when the big day comes and the pages of the big book are turned, it is found that your name is missing. Repent before it is too late.

MAN. Hallelujah! Amen.

BUNTU. Will all those who have not yet handed in their names for membership of our burial society please remain behind.

[*Buntu leaves the pulpit and walks around with a register.*]

Name, please, sir? Number? Thank you.

Good afternoon, sister. Your name, please.

Address? Number? God bless you.

[*He has reached Sizwe.*]

Your name, please, brother?

MAN. Robert Zwelinzima.

BUNTU. Address?

MAN. Fifty, Mapija Street.

BUNTU. N.I. number.

MAN [*again tremendous effort to remember*]. Three . . . eight . . . one . . . one . . . eight . . . six . . . three. . . .

[*They both relax.*]

BUNTU [*after pacing for a few seconds*]. Same man leaving the church . . . walking down the street.

[*Buntu acts out the role while Sizwe watches. He greets other members of the congregation.*]

'God bless you, Brother Bansi. May you always stay within the Lord's mercy.'

'Greetings, Brother Bansi. We welcome you into the flock of Jesus with happy spirits.'

'God bless you, Brother Bansi. Stay with the Lord, the Devil is strong.'

Suddenly. . .

[*Buntu has moved to behind Sizwe. He grabs him roughly by the shoulder.*]

Police!

[*Sizwe stands up frightened. Buntu watches him carefully.*]

No, man! Clean your face.

[*Sizwe adopts an impassive expression. Buntu continues as the policeman.*]

What's your name?

MAN. Robert Zwelinzima.

BUNTU. Where do you work?

MAN. Feltex.

BUNTU. Book!

[*Sizwe hands over the book and waits while the policeman opens it, looks at the photograph, then Sizwe, and finally checks through its stamps and endorsements. While all this is going on Sizwe stands quietly, looking down at his feet, whistling under his breath. The book is finally handed back.*]

Okay.

[*Sizwe takes his book and sits down.*]

MAN [*after a pause*]. I'll try it, Buntu.

BUNTU. Of course you must, if you want to stay alive.

MAN. Yes, but Sizwe Bansi is dead.

BUNTU. What about Robert Zwelinzima then? That poor bastard I pissed on out there in the dark. So *he's* alive again. Bloody miracle, man.

Look, if someone was to offer me the things I wanted most in my life, the things that would make me, my wife, and my child happy, in exchange for the name Buntu . . . you think I wouldn't swop?

MAN. Are you sure, Buntu?

BUNTU [*examining the question seriously*]. If there was just me . . . I mean, if I was alone, if I didn't have anyone to worry about or look after except myself . . . maybe then I'd be prepared to pay some sort of price for a little pride. But if I had a wife and four children wasting away their one and only life in the dust and poverty of Ciskeian Independence . . . if I had four children waiting for me, their father, to do something about their lives . . . *ag*, no, Sizwe. . . .

MAN. Robert, Buntu.

BUNTU [*angry*]. All right! Robert, John, Athol, Winston. . . . Shit on names, man! To hell with them if in exchange you can get a piece of bread for your stomach and a blanket in winter. Understand me, brother, I'm not saying that pride isn't a way for us. What I'm saying is shit on our pride if we only bluff ourselves that we are men.

Take your name back, Sizwe Bansi, if it's so important to you. But next time you hear a white man say 'John' to you, don't say '*Ja, Baas?*' And next time the bloody white man says to you, a man, 'Boy, come here,' don't run to him and lick his arse like we all do. Face him and tell him: 'White man. I'm a Man!' *Ag kak!* We're bluffing ourselves.

It's like my father's hat. Special hat, man! Carefully wrapped in plastic on top of the wardrobe in his room. God help the child who so much as touches it! Sunday it goes on his head, and a man, full of dignity, a man I respect, walks down the street. White man stops him: 'Come here, kaffir!' What does he do?

[*Buntu whips the imaginary hat off his head and crumples it in his hands as he adopts a fawning, servile pose in front of the white man.*]

'What is it, Baas?'

If that is what you call pride, then shit on it! Take mine and give me food for my children.

[*Pause.*]

Look, brother, Robert Zwelinzima, that poor bastard out there in the alleyway, if there *are* ghosts, he is smiling tonight. He is here, with us, and he's saying: 'Good luck, Sizwe! I hope it works.' He's a brother, man.

MAN. For how long, Buntu?

BUNTU. How long? For as long as you can stay out of trouble. Trouble will mean police station, then fingerprints off to Pretoria to check on previous convictions . . . and when they do that . . . Siswe Bansi will live again and you will have had it.

MAN. Buntu, you know what you are saying? A black man stay out of trouble? Impossible, Buntu. Our skin is trouble.

43

BUNTU [*wearily*]. You said you wanted to try.

MAN. And I will.

BUNTU [*picks up his coat*]. I'm tired, . . . Robert. Good luck. See you tomorrow.

[*Exit Buntu, Sizwe picks up the passbook, looks at it for a long time, then puts it in his back pocket. He finds his walking-stick, newspaper, and pipe and moves downstage into a solitary light. He finishes the letter to his wife.*]

MAN. So Nowetu, for the time being my troubles are over. Christmas I come home. In the meantime Buntu is working a plan to get me a Lodger's Permit. If I get it, you and the children can come here and spend some days with me in Port Elizabeth. Spend the money I am sending you carefully. If all goes well I will send some more each week.
I do not forget you, my dear wife.

Your loving Husband,
Sizwe Bansi.

[*As he finishes the letter, Sizwe returns to the pose of the photo. Styles Photographic Studio. Styles is behind the camera.*]

STYLES. Hold it, Robert. Hold it just like that. Just one more. Now smile, Robert. . . . Smile. . . . Smile. . . .

[*Camera flash and blackout.*]

THE ISLAND

CHARACTERS

JOHN
WINSTON   (two prisoners)

This play was given its first performance on 2 July 1973,
directed by Athol Fugard with John Kani as John and Winston
Ntshona as Winston.

SCENE ONE

Centre stage: a raised area representing a cell on Robben Island. Blankets and sleeping-mats—the prisoners sleep on the floor—are neatly folded. In one corner are a bucket of water and two tin mugs.

The long drawn-out wail of a siren. Stage-lights come up to reveal a moat of harsh, white light around the cell. In it the two prisoners— John *stage-right and* Winston *stage-left—mime the digging of sand. They wear the prison uniform of khaki shirt and short trousers. Their heads are shaven. It is an image of back-breaking and grotesquely futile labour. Each in turns fills a wheelbarrow and then with great effort pushes it to where the other man is digging, and empties it. As a result, the piles of sand never diminish. Their labour is interminable. The only sounds are their grunts as they dig, the squeal of the wheel-barrows as they circle the cell, and the hum of Hodoshe, the green carrion fly.*

A whistle is blown. They stop digging and come together, standing side by side as they are handcuffed together and shackled at the ankles. Another whistle. They start to run . . . John mumbling a prayer, Winston muttering a rhythm for their three-legged run.

They do not run fast enough. They get beaten . . . Winston receiving a bad blow to the eye and John spraining an ankle. In this condition they arrive finally at the cell door. Handcuffs and shackles are taken off. After being searched, they lurch into their cell. The door closes behind them. Both men sink to the floor.

A moment of total exhaustion until slowly, painfully, they start to explore their respective injuries . . . Winston his eye, and John his ankle. Winston is moaning softly and this eventually draws John's attention away from his ankle. He crawls to Winston and examines the injured eye. It needs attention. Winston's moaning is slowly turning into a sound of inarticulate outrage, growing in volume and violence. John urinates into one hand and tries to clean the other man's eye with it, but Winston's anger and outrage are now uncontrollable. He breaks away from John and crawls around the cell, blind with rage and pain. John tries to placate him . . . the noise could bring back the warders and still more trouble. Winston eventually finds the cell door but before he can start banging on it John pulls him away.

WINSTON [*calling*]. Hodoshe!

JOHN. Leave him, Winston. Listen to me, man! If he comes now we'll be in bigger shit.

47

WINSTON. I want Hodoshe. I want him now! I want to take him to the office. He must read my warrant. I was sentenced to Life brother, not bloody Death!

JOHN. Please, Winston! He made us run. . . .

WINSTON. I want Hodoshe!

JOHN. He made us run. He's happy now. Leave him. Maybe he'll let us go back to the quarry tomorrow. . . .

[*Winston is suddenly silent. For a moment John thinks his words are having an effect, but then he realizes that the other man is looking at his ear. Winston touches it. It is bleeding. A sudden spasm of fear from John who puts a hand to his ear. His fingers come away with blood on them. The two men look at each other.*]

WINSTON. *Nyana we Sizwe!*

[*In a reversal of earlier roles Winston now gets John down on the floor of the cell so as to examine the injured ear. He has to wipe blood and sweat out of his eyes in order to see clearly. John winces with pain. Winston keeps restraining him.*]

WINSTON [*eventually*]. It's not too bad. [*Using his shirt-tail he cleans the injured ear.*]

JOHN [*through clenched teeth as Winston tends his ear*]. Hell, *ons was gemoer vandag!* [*A weak smile.*] News bulletin and weather forecast! Black Domination was chased by White Domination. Black Domination lost its shoes and collected a few bruises. Black Domination will run barefoot to the quarry tomorrow. Conditions locally remain unchanged—thunderstorms with the possibility of cold showers and rain. Elsewhere, fine and warm!

[*Winston has now finished tending John's ear and settles down on the floor beside him. He clears his nose, ears, and eyes of sand.*]

WINSTON. Sand! Same old sea sand I used to play with when I was young. St George's Strand. New Year's Day. Sand dunes. Sand castles. . . .

JOHN. *Ja;* we used to go there too. Last. . . . [*Pause and then a small laugh. He shakes his head.*] The Christmas before they arrested me, we were down there. All of us. Honeybush. My little Monde played in the sand. We'd given her one of those little buckets and spades for Christmas.

WINSTON. *Ja.*

JOHN. Anyway, it was Daddy's turn today. [*Shaking his head ruefully.*] *Haai*, Winston, this one goes on the record. 'Struesgod! I'm a man, brother. A man! But if Hodoshe had kept us at those wheelbarrows five minutes longer . . . ! There would have been a baby on the Island tonight. I nearly cried.

WINSTON. *Ja.*

JOHN. There was no end to it, except one of us!

WINSTON. That's right.

JOHN. This morning when he said: 'You two! The beach!' . . . I thought, Okay, so it's my turn to empty the sea into a hole. He likes that one. But when he pointed to the wheelbarrows, and I saw his idea . . . ! [*Shaking his head.*] I laughed at first. Then I wasn't laughing. Then I hated you. You looked so stupid, *broer!*

WINSTON. That's what he wanted.

JOHN. It was going to last forever, man! Because of *you*. And for *you*, because of *me*. *Moer!* He's cleverer than I thought.

WINSTON. If he was God, he would have done it.

JOHN. What?

WINSTON. Broken us. Men get tired. Hey! There's a thought. We're still alive because Hodoshe got tired.

JOHN. Tomorrow?

WINSTON. We'll see.

JOHN. If he takes us back there . . . If I hear that wheelbarrow . . . of yours again, coming with another bloody load of . . . eternity!

WINSTON [*with calm resignation*]. We'll see.

[*Pause. John looks at Winston.*]

JOHN [*with quiet emphasis, as if the other man did not fully understand the significance of what he had said*]. I *hated* you Winston.

WINSTON [*meeting John's eyes*]. *I* hated *you*.

[*John puts a hand on Winston's shoulder. Their brotherhood is intact. He gets slowly to his feet.*]

JOHN. Where's the *lap?*

WINSTON. Somewhere. Look for it.

JOHN. Hey! You had it last.

49

[Limping around the cell looking for their washrag.]

WINSTON. *Haai*, man! You got no wife here. Look for the rag yourself.

JOHN *[finding the rag beside the water bucket]*. Look where it is. Look! Hodoshe comes in here and sees it. 'Whose *lappie* is that?' Then what do you say?

WINSTON. 'It's his rag, sir.'

JOHN. Yes? Okay. 'It's my rag, sir.' When you wash, use your shirt.

WINSTON. Okay, okay! 'It's our rag, sir!'

JOHN. That will be the bloody day!

[John, getting ready to wash, starts to take off his shirt. Winston produces a cigarette butt, matches, and flint from their hiding-place under the water bucket. He settles down for a smoke.]

Shit, today was long. Hey, Winston, suppose the watch of the chap behind the siren is slow! We could still be there, man! *[He pulls out three or four rusty nails from a secret pocket in his trousers. He holds them out to Winston.]* Hey there.

WINSTON. What?

JOHN. With the others.

WINSTON *[taking the nails]*. What's this?

JOHN. Necklace, man. With the others.

WINSTON. Necklace?

JOHN. Antigone's necklace.

WINSTON. *Ag*, shit, man!

[Slams the nails down on the cell floor and goes on smoking.]

Antigone! Go to hell, man, John.

JOHN. Hey, don't start any nonsense now. You promised. *[Limps over to Winston's bed-roll and produces a half-completed necklace made of nails and string.]* It's nearly finished. Look. Three fingers, one nail ... three fingers, one nail.... *[Places the necklace beside Winston who is shaking his head, smoking aggressively, and muttering away.]* Don't start any nonsense now, Winston. There's six days to go to the concert. We're committed. We promised the chaps we'd do something. This *Antigone* is just right for us. Six more days and we'll make it.

[He continues washing.]

WINSTON. Jesus, John! We were down on the beach today. Hodoshe made us run. Can't you just leave a man . . . ?

JOHN. To hell with you! Who do you think ran with you? I'm also tired, but we can't back out now. Come on! Three fingers. . . .

WINSTON. . . . one nail! [*Shaking his head.*] *Haai . . . haai . . . haai!*

JOHN. Stop moaning and get on with it. Shit, Winston! What sort of progress is this? [*Abandoning his wash.*] Listen. Listen! Number 42 is practising the Zulu War Dance. Down there they're rehearsing their songs. It's just in this *moer* cell that there's always an argument. Today you want to do it, tomorrow you don't want to do it. How the hell must I know what to report to the chaps tomorrow if we go back to the quarry?

[*Winston is unyielding. His obstinacy gets the better of John, who eventually throws the wash-rag at him.*]

There! Wash!

[*John applies himself to the necklace while Winston, still muttering away in an undertone, starts to clean himself.*]

How can I be sure of anything when you carry on like this? We've still got to learn the words, the moves. Shit! It could be so bloody good, man.

[*Winston mutters protests all the way through this speech of John's. The latter holds up the necklace.*]

Nearly finished! Look at it! Three fingers. . . .

WINSTON. . . . one nail.

JOHN. *Ja!* Simple. Do you still remember all I told you yesterday? Bet you've bloody forgotten. How can I carry on like this? I can't move on, man. Over the whole bloody lot again! Who Antigone is . . . who Creon is. . . .

WINSTON. Antigone is mother to Polynices. . . .

JOHN. *Haai, haai, haai* . . . shit, Winston! [*Now really exasperated.*] How many times must I tell you that Antigone is the sister to the two brothers? Not the mother. That's another play.

WINSTON. Oh.

JOHN. That's all you know! 'Oh.' [*He abandons the necklace and*

51

fishes out a piece of chalk from a crack in the floor.] Come here. This is the last time. 'Struesgod. The last time.

WINSTON. *Ag,* no, John.

JOHN. Come! I'm putting this plot down for the last time! If you don't learn it tonight I'm going to report you to the old men tomorrow. And remember, *broer,* those old men will make Hodoshe and his tricks look like a little boy.

WINSTON. Jesus Christ! Learn to dig for Hodoshe, learn to run for Hodoshe, and what happens when I get back to the cell? Learn to read *Antigone!*

JOHN. Come! And shut up! [*He pulls the reluctant Winston down beside him on the floor. Winston continues to clean himself with the rag while John lays out the 'plot' of Antigone.*] If you would just stop moaning, you would learn faster. Now listen!

WINSTON. Okay, do it.

JOHN. Listen! It is the Trial of Antigone. Right?

WINSTON. So you say.

JOHN. First, the accused. Who is the accused?

WINSTON. Antigone.

JOHN. Coming from you that's bloody progress. [*Writing away on the cell floor with his chalk.*] Next the State. Who is the State?

WINSTON. Creon.

JOHN. King Creon. Creon is the State. Now . . . what did Antigone do?

WINSTON. Antigone buried her brother Eteocles.

JOHN. No, no, no! Shit, Winston, when are you going to remember this thing? I told you, man, Antigone buried Polynices. The traitor! The one who I said was on *our* side. Right?

WINSTON. Right.

JOHN. Stage one of the Trial. [*Writing on the floor.*] The State lays its charges against the Accused . . . and lists counts . . . you know the way they do it. Stage two is Pleading. What does Antigone plead? Guilty or Not Guilty?

WINSTON. Not Guilty.

JOHN [*trying to be tactful*]. Now look, Winston, we're not going to argue. Between me and you, in this cell, we know she's

Not Guilty. But in the play she pleads Guilty.

WINSTON. No, man, John! Antigone is Not Guilty. . . .

JOHN. In the play. . . .

WINSTON [*losing his temper*]. To hell with the play! Antigone had every right to bury her brother.

JOHN. Don't say 'To hell with the play'. We've got to do the bloody thing. And in the play she pleads Guilty. Get that straight. Antigone pleads. . . .

WINSTON [*giving up in disgust*]. Okay, do it your way.

JOHN. It's not my way! In the play. . . .

WINSTON. Guilty!

JOHN. Yes, Guilty!

[*Writes furiously on the floor.*]

WINSTON. Guilty.

JOHN. Stage three, Pleading in Mitigation of Sentence. Stage four, Sentence, State Summary, and something from you . . . Farewell Words. Now learn that.

WINSTON. Hey?

JOHN [*getting up*]. Learn that!

WINSTON. But we've just done it!

JOHN. *I've* just done it. Now *you* learn it.

WINSTON [*throwing aside the wash-rag with disgust before applying himself to learning the 'plot'*]. Learn to run, learn to read. . . .

JOHN. And don't throw the rag there! [*Retrieving the rag and placing it in its correct place.*] Don't be so bloody difficult, man. We're nearly there. You'll be proud of this thing when we've done it.

[*Limps to his bed-roll and produces a pendant made from a jam-tin lid and twine.*] Look. Winston, look! Creon's medallion. Good, hey! [*Hangs it around his neck.*] I'll finish the necklace while you learn that.

[*He strings on the remaining nails.*] Jesus, Winston! June 1965.

WINSTON. What?

JOHN. This, man. *Antigone*. In New Brighton. St. Stephen's Hall. The place was packed, man! All the big people. Front row . . . dignitaries. Shit, those were the days. Georgie was Creon. You know Georgie?

WINSTON. The teacher?

JOHN. That's him. He played Creon. Should have seen him, Winston. Short and fat, with big eyes, but by the time the play was finished he was as tall as the roof.

[*Onto his legs in an imitation of Georgie's Creon.*]

'My Councillors, now that the Gods have brought our City safe through a storm of troubles to tranquillity. . . .' And old Mulligan! Another short-arsed teacher. With a beard! He used to go up to the Queen. . . . [*Another imitation.*] 'Your Majesty, prepare for grief, but do not weep.'

[*The necklace in his hands.*]

Nearly finished!

Nomhle played Antigone. A bastard of a lady that one, but a beautiful bitch. Can't get her out of my mind tonight.

WINSTON [*indicating the 'plot'*]. I know this.

JOHN. You sure?

WINSTON. This! . . . it's here. [*Tapping his head.*]

JOHN. You're not bullshitting, hey? [*He rubs out the 'plot' and then paces the cell.*] Right. The Trial of Antigone. Who is the Accused?

WINSTON. Antigone.

JOHN. Who is the State?

WINSTON. King Creon.

JOHN. Stage one.

WINSTON [*supremely self-confident*]. Antigone lays charges. . . .

JOHN. NO, SHIT, MAN, WINSTON!!!

[*Winston pulls John down and stifles his protests with a hand over his mouth.*]

WINSTON. Okay . . . okay . . . listen, John . . . listen. . . . The State lays charges against Antigone.

[*Pause.*]

JOHN. Be careful!

WINSTON. The State lays charges against Antigone.

JOHN. Stage two.

WINSTON. Pleading.

JOHN. What does she plead? Guilty or Not Guilty?

Winston and John.

WINSTON. Guilty.

JOHN. Stage three.

WINSTON. Pleading in Mitigation of Sentence.

JOHN. Stage four.

WINSTON. State Summary, Sentence, and Farewell Words.

JOHN [*very excited*]. He's got it! That's my man. See how easy it is, Winston? Tomorrow, just the words.

[*Winston gets onto his legs, John puts away the props. Mats and blankets are unrolled. The two men prepare for sleep.*]

JOHN. Hell, I hope we go back to the quarry tomorrow. There's still a lot of things we need for props and costumes. Your wig! The boys in Number Fourteen said they'd try and smuggle me a piece of rope from the jetty.

WINSTON. *Ja*, I hope we're back there. I want to try and get some tobacco through to Sipho.

JOHN. Sipho?

WINSTON. Back in solitary.

JOHN. Again!

WINSTON. *Ja*.

JOHN. Oh hell!

WINSTON. Simon passed the word.

JOHN. What was it this time?

WINSTON. Complained about the food I think. Demanded to see the book of Prison Regulations.

JOHN. Why don't they leave him alone for a bit?

WINSTON. Because he doesn't leave them alone.

JOHN. You're right. I'm glad I'm not in Number Twenty-two with him. One man starts getting hard-arsed like that and the whole lot of you end up in the shit.

[*Winston's bed is ready. He lies down.*]

You know what I'm saying?

WINSTON. *Ja*.

JOHN. What?

WINSTON. What 'What'?

JOHN. What am I saying?

WINSTON. *Haai,* Johnny, man! I'm tired now! Let a man. . . .

JOHN. I'm saying Don't Be Hard-Arsed! You! When Hodoshe opens that door tomorrow say '*Ja, Baas*' the right way. I don't want to be back on that bloody beach tomorrow just because you feel like being difficult.

WINSTON [*wearily*]. Okay, man, Johnny.

JOHN. You're not alone in this cell. I'm here too.

WINSTON. Jesus, you think I don't know that!

JOHN. People must remember their responsibilities to others.

WINSTON. I'm glad to hear you say that, because I was just going to remind you that it is your turn tonight.

JOHN. What do you mean? Wasn't it my turn last night?

WINSTON [*shaking his head emphatically*]. Haai, haai. Don't you remember? Last night I took you to bioscope.

JOHN. Hey, by the way! So you did. Bloody good film too. 'Fastest Gun in the West'. Glenn Ford.

[*Whips out a six-shooter and guns down a few bad-men.*]

You were bullshitting me a bit though. How the hell can Glenn Ford shoot backwards through his legs. I tried to work that one out on the beach.

[*He is now seated on his bed-roll. After a moment's thought he holds up an empty mug as a telephone-receiver and starts to dial. Winston watches him with puzzlement.*]

Operator, put me through to New Brighton, please . . . yes, New Brighton, Port Elizabeth. The number is 414624. . . . Yes, mine is local . . . local. . . .

WINSTON [*recognizing the telephone number*]. The Shop!

[*He sits upright with excitement as John launches into the telephone conversation.*]

JOHN. That you Scott? Hello, man! Guess who! . . . You got it! You bastard! Hell, shit, Scott, man . . . how things with you? No, still inside. Give me the news, man . . . you don't say! No, we don't hear anything here . . . not a word. . . . What's that? Business is bad? . . . You bloody undertaker! People aren't dying fast enough! No, things are fine here. . . .

[*Winston, squirming with excitement, has been trying unsuccessfully*] *to interrupt John's torrent of words and laughter. He finally succeeds in drawing John's attention.*]

WINSTON. Who else is there? Who's with Scott?

JOHN. Hey, Scott, who's there with you?...Oh no!...call him to the phone, man. . . .

WINSTON. Who's it?

JOHN [*ignoring Winston*]. Just for a minute, man, please, Scott. . . .

[*Ecstatic response from John as another voice comes over the phone.*]

Hello there, you beautiful bastard . . . how's it, man? . . .

WINSTON. Who the hell is it, man?

JOHN [*hand over the receiver*]. Sky!

[*Winston can no longer contain his excitement. He scrambles out of his bed to join John, and joins in the fun with questions and remarks whispered into John's ear. Both men enjoy it enormously.*]

How's it with Mangi? Where's Vusi? How are the chaps keeping, Sky? Winston? . . . All right, man. He's here next to me. No, fine, man, fine, man . . . small accident today when he collided with Hodoshe, but nothing to moan about. His right eye bruised, that's all. Hey, Winston's asking how are the punkies doing? [*Big laugh.*] You bloody lover boy! Leave something for us, man!

[*John becomes aware of Winston trying to interrupt again: to Winston.*]

Okay . . . okay. . . .

[*Back to the telephone.*] Listen, Sky, Winston says if you get a chance, go down to Dora Street, to his wife. Tell V. Winston says he's okay, things are fine. Winston says she must carry on . . . nothing has happened . . . tell her to take care of everything and everybody. . . . Ja. . . .

[*The mention of his wife guillotines Winston's excitement and fun. After a few seconds of silence he crawls back heavily to his bed and lies down. A similar shift in mood takes place in John.*]

And look, Sky, you're not far from Gratten Street. Cross over to it, man, drop in on number thirty-eight, talk to Princess, my wife. How is she keeping? Ask her for me. I haven't received a letter for three months now. Why aren't they writing? Tell her to write, man. I want to know how the children are keeping. Is Monde still at school? How's my twin baby, my Father and Mother? Is the old girl sick? They mustn't be afraid to tell me. I want to know. I know it's an effort to write, but it means a lot to us here. Tell her . . . this was another day. They're not very different here. We were down on the beach. The wind was blowing. The sand got in our eyes. The sea was rough. I couldn't see the mainland properly. Tell them that maybe tomorrow we'll go to the quarry. It's not so bad there. We'll be with the others. Tell her also . . . it's starting to get cold now, but the worst is still coming.

[*Slow fade to blackout.*]

SCENE TWO

The cell, a few days later.
John is hidden under a blanket. Winston is in the process of putting on Antigone's wig and false breasts.

JOHN. Okay?

WINSTON [*still busy*]. No.

JOHN. Okay?

WINSTON. No.

JOHN. Okay?

WINSTON. No.

[*Pause*]

JOHN. Okay?

[*Winston is ready. He stands waiting. John slowly lifts the blanket and looks. He can't believe his eyes. Winston is a very funny sight. John's amazement turns into laughter, which builds steadily. He bangs on the cell wall.*]

Hey, Norman. Norman! Come this side, man. I got it here. *Poes!*

[*John launches into an extravagant send-up of Winston's Antigone. He circles 'her' admiringly, he fondles her breasts, he walks arm in arm with her down Main Street, collapsing with laughter between each 'turn'. He climaxes everything by dropping his trousers.*]

Speedy Gonzales! Here I come!

[*This last joke is too much for Winston who has endured the whole performance with mounting but suppressed anger. He tears off the wig and breasts, throws them down on the cell floor, and storms over to the water bucket where he starts to clean himself.*]

WINSTON. It's finished! I'm not doing it. Take your Antigone and shove it up your arse!

JOHN [*trying to control himself*]. Wait, man. Wait. . . .

[*He starts laughing again.*]

WINSTON. There is nothing to wait for, my friend. I'm not doing it.

JOHN. Please, Winston!

WINSTON. You can laugh as much as you like, my friend, but

just let's get one thing straight, I'm *not* doing Antigone. And in case you want to know why . . . I'm a man, not a bloody woman.

JOHN. When did I say otherwise?

WINSTON. What were you laughing at?

JOHN. I'm not laughing now.

WINSTON. What are you doing, crying?

[*Another burst of laughter from John.*]

There you go again, more laughing! Shit, man, you want me to go out there tomorrow night and make a bloody fool of myself? You think I don't know what will happen after that? Every time I run to the quarry . . . 'Nyah . . . nyah. . . . Here comes Antigone! . . . Help the poor lady! . . .' Well, you can go to hell with your Antigone.

JOHN. I wasn't laughing at you.

WINSTON. Then who were you laughing at? Who else was here that dressed himself as a lady and made a bloody fool of himself?

JOHN [*now trying very hard to placate the other man*]. Okay Winston, Okay! I'm not laughing any more.

WINSTON. You can go to hell with what you're saying.

JOHN. Look, Winston, try to understand, man, . . . this is Theatre.

WINSTON. You call laughing at me Theatre? Then go to hell with your Theatre!

JOHN. Please, Winston, just stop talking and listen to me.

WINSTON. No! You get this, brother, . . . I am not doing your Antigone! I would rather run the whole day for Hodoshe. At least I know where I stand with him. All *he* wants is to make me a 'boy' . . . not a bloody woman.

JOHN. Okay, okay. . . .

WINSTON. Nothing you can say. . . .

JOHN [*shouting the other man down*]. Will you bloody listen!

WINSTON [*throwing the wash-rag down violently*]. Okay. I'm listening.

JOHN. Sure I laughed. *Ja . . . I laughed.* But can I tell you why I laughed? I was preparing you for . . . stage fright! You

John and Winston.

think I don't know what I'm doing in this cell? This is preparation for stage fright! I know those bastards out there. When you get in front of them, sure they'll laugh . . . Nyah, nyah! . . . they'll laugh. But just remember this brother, nobody laughs forever! There'll come a time when they'll stop laughing, and that will be the time when our Antigone hits them with her words.

WINSTON. You're day-dreaming, John. Just get it into your head that I'm not doing Antigone. It's as simple as that.

JOHN [*realizing for the first time that Winston needs to be handled very carefully*]. Hey, Winston! Hold on there, man. We've only got one more day to go! They've given us the best spot in the programme. We end the show! You can't back out now.

WINSTON. You think I can't? Just wait and see.

JOHN. Winston! You want to get me into trouble? Is that what you want?

WINSTON. Okay, I won't back out.

JOHN [*delighted with his easy victory*]. That's my man!

WINSTON [*retrieving the wig and false breasts off the floor and slamming them into John's hands*]. Here's Antigone . . . take these titties and hair and play Antigone. I'm going to play Creon. Do you understand what I'm saying? Take your two titties. . . . I'll have my balls and play Creon. [*Turns his back on a flabbergasted John, fishes out a cigarette-butt and matches from under the water bucket, and settles down for a smoke.*]

JOHN [*after a stunned silence*]. You won't make it! I thought about that one days ago. It's too late now to learn Creon's words.

WINSTON [*smoking*]. I hate to say it, but that is just too bad. I am not doing Antigone.

[*John is now furious. After a moment's hesitation he stuffs on the wig and false breasts and confronts Winston.*]

JOHN. Look at me. Now laugh.

[*Winston tries, but the laugh is forced and soon dies away.*]

Go on.

[*Pause.*]

Go on laughing! Why did you stop? Must I tell you why?

Because behind all this rubbish is me, and you know it's me. You think those bastards out there won't know it's you? Yes, they'll laugh. But who cares about that as long as they laugh in the beginning and listen at the end. That's all we want them to do . . . listen at the end!

WINSTON. I don't care what you say John. I'm not doing Antigone.

JOHN. Winston . . . you're being difficult. You promised. . . .

WINSTON. Go to hell, man. Only last night you tell me that this Antigone is a bloody . . . what you call it . . . legend! A Greek one at that. Bloody thing never even happened. Not even history! Look, brother, I got no time for bullshit. Fuck legends. Me? . . . I live my life here! I know why I'm here, and it's history, not legends. I had my chat with a magistrate in Cradock and now I'm here. Your Antigone is a child's play, man.

JOHN. Winston! That's Hodoshe's talk.

WINSTON. You can go to hell with that one too.

JOHN. Hodoshe's talk, Winston! That's what he says all the time. What he wants us to say all our lives. Our convictions, our ideals . . . that's what he calls them . . . child's play. Everything we fucking do is 'child's play' . . . when we ran that whole day in the sun and pushed those wheelbarrows, when we cry, when we shit . . . child's play! Look, brother, . . . I've had enough. No one is going to stop me doing Antigone. . . .

[*The two men break apart suddenly, drop their trousers, and stand facing the wall with arms outstretched. Hodoshe calls John.*]
Yes, sir!
[*He then pulls up his trousers and leaves the cell. When he has left, Winston pulls up his trousers and starts muttering with savage satisfaction at the thought of John in Hodoshe's hands.*]

WINSTON. There he goes. Serves him right. I just hope Hodoshe teaches him a lesson. Antigone is important! Antigone this! Antigone that! Shit, man. Nobody can sleep in this bloody cell because of all that bullshit. Polynices! Eteocles! The other prisoners too. Nobody gets any peace and quiet because of that bloody Antigone! I hope Hodoshe gives it to him.

[*He is now at the cell door. He listens, then moves over to the wig on the floor and circles it. He finally picks it up. Moves back to the cell door to make sure no one is coming. The water bucket gives him an idea. He puts on the wig and, after some difficulty, manages to see his reflection in the water. A good laugh, which he cuts off abruptly. He moves around the cell trying out a few of Antigone's poses. None of them work. He feels a fool. He finally tears off the wig and throws it down on the floor with disgust.]*

Ag voetsek!

[Hands in pockets he paces the cell with grim determination.]

I'm not going to do it. And I'm going to tell him. When he comes back. For once he must just shut that big bloody mouth of his and listen. To me! I'm not going to argue, but 'struesgod that . . . !

[The wig on the floor. He stamps on it.]

Shit, man! If he wants a woman in the cell he must send for his wife, and I don't give a damn how he does it. I didn't walk with those men and burn my bloody passbook in front of that police station, and have a magistrate send me here for life so that he can dress me up like a woman and make a bloody fool of me. I'm going to tell him. When he walks through that door.

[John returns. Winston is so involved in the problem of Antigone that at first he does not register John's strangely vacant manner.]

Listen, *broer,* I'm not trying to be difficult but this Antigone! No! Please listen to me, John. 'Struesgod I can't do it. I mean, let's try something else, like singing or something. You always got ideas. You know I can sing or dance. But not Antigone. Please, John.

JOHN [*quietly*]. Winston. . . .

WINSTON [*still blind to the other man's manner*]. Don't let's argue, man. We've been together in this cell too long now to quarrel about rubbish. But you know me. If there's one thing I can't stand it's people laughing at me. If I go out there tomorrow night and those bastards start laughing I'll fuck up the first one I lay my hands on. You saw yourself what happened in here when you started laughing. I wanted to *moer* you, John. I'm not joking. I really wanted to. . . . Hey, are you listening to me? [*Looking squarely at John.*]

JOHN. Winston . . . I've got something to tell you.

WINSTON [*registering John's manner for the first time*]. What's the matter? Hodoshe? What happened? Are we in shit? Solitary?

JOHN. My appeal was heard last Wednesday. Sentence reduced. I've got three months to go.

[*Long silence. Winston is stunned. Eventually. . . .*]

WINSTON. Three. . . .

JOHN. . . . months to go.

WINSTON. Three. . . .

JOHN. *Ja*. That's what Prinsloo said.

WINSTON. John!

[*Winston explodes with joy. The men embrace. They dance a jig in the cell. Winston finally tears himself away and starts to hammer on the cell walls so as to pass on the news to other prisoners.*]

Norman! Norman!! John. Three months to go. *Ja*. . . . Just been told. . . .

[*Winston's excitement makes John nervous. He pulls Winston away from the wall.*]

JOHN. Winston! Not yet, man. We'll tell them at the quarry tomorrow. Let me just live with it for a little while.

WINSTON. Okay okay. . . . How did it happen?

[*He pulls John down to the floor. They sit close together.*]

JOHN. Jesus, I'm so mixed up, man! *Ja* . . . the door opened and I saw Hodoshe. Ooo God, I said to myself. Trouble! Here we go again! All because of you and the noise you were making. Went down the corridor straight to Number Four . . . Solitary and Spare Diet!! But at the end, instead of turning right, we turned left into the main block, all the way through it to Prinsloo's office.

WINSTON. Prinsloo!

JOHN. I'm telling you. Prinsloo himself, man. We waited outside for a little bit, then Hodoshe pushed me in. Prinsloo was behind his desk, busy with some papers. He pulled out one and said to me: 'You are very lucky. Your lawyers have been working on your case. The sentence has been reduced from ten years, to three.'

WINSTON. What did Hodoshe say?

JOHN. Nothing. But he looked unhappy.

[*They laugh.*]

64

Hey, something else. Hodoshe let me walk back here by myself! He didn't follow me.

WINSTON. Of course. You are free.

JOHN. *Haai*, Winston, not yet. Those three months . . . ! Or suppose it's a trick.

WINSTON. What do you mean?

JOHN. Those bastards will do anything to break you. If the wheelbarrows and the quarry don't do it, they'll try something else. Remember that last visit of wives, when they lined up all the men on the other side. . . . 'Take a good look and say goodbye! Back to the cells!'

WINSTON. You say you saw Prinsloo?

JOHN. Prinsloo himself. Bastard didn't even stand up when I walked in. And by the way . . . I had to sign. *Ja!* I had to sign a form to say that I had been officially told of the result of my appeal . . . that I had three months to go. *Ja.* I signed!

WINSTON [*without the slightest doubt*]. It's three months, John.

JOHN [*relaxing and living with the reality for the first time*]. Hell, Winston, at the end of those three months, it will be three years together in this cell. Three years ago I stood in front of that magistrate at Kirkwood—bastard didn't even look at me: 'Ten years!' I watched ten years of my life drift away like smoke from a cigarette while he fidgeted and scratched his arse. That same night back in the prison van to the cells at Rooihel. First time we met!

WINSTON. *Ja.* We had just got back from our trial in Cradock.

JOHN. You, Temba, . . .

WINSTON. Sipho. . . .

JOHN. Hell, man!

WINSTON. First time we got close to each other was the next morning in the yard, when they lined us up for the vans. . . .

JOHN. And married us!

[*They lock left and right hands together to suggest handcuffs.*]

WINSTON. Who was that old man . . . remember him? . . . in the corner handcuffed to Sipho?

65

JOHN. Sipho?

WINSTON. *Ja*, the one who started the singing.

JOHN [*remembering*]. Peter. Tatu Peter.

WINSTON. That's him!

JOHN. Hell, it comes back now, man! Pulling through the big gates, wives and mothers running next to the vans, trying to say goodbye . . . all of us inside fighting for a last look through the window.

WINSTON [*shaking his head*]. Shit!

JOHN. Bet you've forgotten the song the old man started?

[*Winston tries to remember. John starts singing softly. It is one of the Defiance Campaign songs. Winston joins in.*]

WINSTON [*shaking his head ruefully*]. By the time we reach Humansdorp though, nobody was singing.

JOHN. Fuck singing. I wanted to piss. Hey! I had my one free hand on my balls, holding on. I'd made a mistake when we left the Rooihel. Drank a gallon of water thinking of those five hundred miles ahead. Jesus! There was the bucket in the corner! But we were packed in so tight, remember, we couldn't move. I tried to pull you but it was no bloody good. So I held on—Humansdorp, Storms River, Blaaukrantz . . . held on. But at Knysna, to hell with it, I let go!

[*Gesture to indicate the release of his bladder. Winston finds this enormously funny. John joins in.*]

You were also wet by then!

WINSTON. Never!

JOHN. Okay, let's say that by George nobody was dry. Remember the stop there?

WINSTON. *Ja*. I thought they were going to let us walk around a bit.

JOHN. Not a damn! Fill up with petrol and then on. Hey, but what about those locals, the Coloured prisoners, when we pulled away. Remember? Coming to their cell windows and shouting . . . 'Courage, Brothers! Courage!' After that . . . ! Jesus, I was tired. Didn't we fall asleep? Standing like that?

WINSTON. What do you mean standing? It was impossible to fall.

JOHN. Then the docks, the boat. . . . It was my first time on one. I had nothing to vomit up, but my God I tried.

WINSTON. What about me?

JOHN. Then we saw this place for the first time. It almost looked pretty, hey, with all the mist around it.

WINSTON. I was too sick to see anything, *broer.*

JOHN. Remember your words when we jumped off onto the jetty?

[*Pause. The two men look at each other.*]

Heavy words, Winston. You looked back at the mountains . . . 'Farewell Africa!' I've never forgotten them. That was three years ago.

WINSTON. And now, for you, it's three months to go.

[*Pause. The mood of innocent celebration has passed. John realizes what his good news means to the other man.*]

JOHN. To hell with everything. Let's go to bed.

[*Winston doesn't move. John finds Antigone's wig.*]

We'll talk about Antigone tomorrow.

[*John prepares for bed.*]

Hey, Winston! I just realized. My family! Princess and the children. Do you think they've been told? Jesus, man, maybe they're also saying . . . three months! Those three months are going to feel as long as the three years. Time passes slowly when you've got something . . . to wait for. . . .

[*Pause. Winston still hasn't moved. John changes his tone.*]

Look, in this cell we're going to forget those three months. The whole bloody thing is most probably a trick anyway. So let's just forget about it. We run to the quarry tomorrow. Together. So let's sleep.

SCENE THREE

The cell, later the same night. Both men are in bed. Winston is apparently asleep. John, however, is awake, rolling restlessly from side to side. He eventually gets up and goes quietly to the bucket for a drink of water, then back to his bed. He doesn't lie down, however. Pulling the blanket around his shoulders he starts to think about the three months. He starts counting the days on the fingers of one hand. Behind him Winston sits up and watches him in silence for a few moments.

WINSTON [*with a strange smile*]. You're counting!

JOHN [*with a start*]. What! Hey, Winston, you gave me a fright, man. I thought you were asleep. What's the matter? Can't you sleep?

WINSTON [*ignoring the question, still smiling*]. You've started counting the days now.

JOHN [*unable to resist the temptation to talk, moving over to Winston's bed*]. *Ja.*

WINSTON. How many?

JOHN. Ninety-two.

WINSTON. You see!

JOHN [*excited*]. Simple, man. Look . . . twenty days left in this month, thirty days in June, thirty-one in July, eleven days in August . . . ninety-two.

WINSTON [*still smiling, but watching John carefully*]. Tomorrow?

JOHN. Ninety-one.

WINSTON. And the next day?

JOHN. Ninety.

WINSTON. Then one day it will be eighty!

JOHN. *Ja!*

WINSTON. Then seventy.

JOHN. Hey, Winston, time doesn't pass so fast.

WINSTON. Then only sixty more days.

JOHN. That's just two months here on the Island.

WINSTON. Fifty . . . forty days in the quarry.

JOHN. Jesus, Winston!

WINSTON. Thirty.

JOHN. One month. Only one month to go.

WINSTON. Twenty . . . [*holding up his hands*] then ten . . . five, four, three, two . . . tomorrow!

[*The anticipation of that moment is too much for John.*]

JOHN. NO! Please, man, Winston. It hurts. Leave those three months alone. I'm going to sleep!

[*Back to his bed where he curls up in a tight ball and tries determinedly to sleep. Winston lies down again and stares up at the ceiling. After a pause he speaks quietly.*]

WINSTON. They won't keep you here for the full three months. Only two months. Then down to the jetty, into a ferry-boat . . . you'll say goodbye to this place . . . and straight to Victor Verster Prison on the mainland.

[*Against his will John starts to listen. He eventually sits upright and completely surrenders himself to Winston's description of the last few days of his confinement.*]

Life will change for you there. It will be much easier. Because you won't take Hodoshe with you. He'll stay here with me, on the Island. They'll put you to work in the vineyards at Victor Verster, John. There are no quarries there. Eating grapes, oranges . . . they'll change your diet . . . Diet C, and exercises so that you'll look good when they let you out finally. At night you'll play games . . . Ludo, draughts, snakes and ladders! Then one day they'll call you into the office, with a van waiting outside to take you back. The same five hundred miles. But this time they'll let you sit. You won't have to stand the whole way like you did coming here. And there won't be handcuffs. Maybe they'll even stop on the way so that you can have a pee. Yes, I'm sure they will. You might even sleep over somewhere. Then finally Port Elizabeth. Rooihel Prison again, John! That's very near home, man. New Brighton is next door! Through your cell window you'll see people moving up and down in the street, hear the buses roaring. Then one night you won't sleep again, because you'll be counting. Not days, as you are doing now, but hours. And the next morning, that beautiful morning, John,

69

they'll take you straight out of your cell to the Discharge Office where they'll give you a new khaki shirt, long khaki trousers, brown shoes. And your belongings! I almost forgot your belongings.

JOHN. Hey, by the way! I was wearing a white shirt, black tie, grey flannel trousers . . . brown Crockett shoes . . . socks? [*A little laugh.*] I can't remember my socks! A check jacket . . . and my watch! I was wearing my watch!

WINSTON. They'll wrap them up in a parcel. You'll have it under your arm when they lead you to the gate. And outside, John, outside that gate, New Brighton will be waiting for you. Your mother, your father, Princess and the children . . . and when they open it. . . .

[*Once again, but more violently this time, John breaks the mood as the anticipation of the moment of freedom becomes too much for him.*]

JOHN. Stop it, Winston! Leave those three months alone for Christ's sake. I want to sleep.

[*He tries to get away from Winston, but the latter goes after him. Winston has now also abandoned his false smile.*]

WINSTON [*stopping John as he tries to crawl away*]. But it's not finished, John!

JOHN. Leave me alone!

WINSTON. It doesn't end there. Your people will take you home. Thirty-eight, Gratten Street, John! Remember it? Everybody will be waiting for you . . . aunts, uncles, friends, neighbours. They'll put you in a chair, John, like a king, give you anything you want . . . cakes, sweets, cooldrinks . . . and then you'll start to talk. You'll tell them about this place, John, about Hodoshe, about the quarry, and about your good friend Winston who you left behind. But you still won't be happy, hey. Because you'll need a fuck. A really wild one!

JOHN. Stop it, Winston!

WINSTON [*relentless*]. And that is why at ten o'clock that night you'll slip out through the back door and make your way to Sky's place. Imagine it, man! All the boys waiting for you . . . Georgie, Mangi, Vusumzi. They'll fill you up with booze. They'll look after you. They know what it's like inside. They'll fix you up with a woman. . . .

JOHN. NO!

WINSTON. Set you up with her in a comfortable joint, and then leave you alone. You'll watch her, watch her take her clothes off, you'll take your pants off, get near her, feel her, feel it. . . . Ja, you'll feel it. It will be wet. . . .

JOHN. WINSTON!

WINSTON. Wet *poes*, John! And you'll fuck it wild!

[*John turns finally to face Winston. A long silence as the two men confront each other. John is appalled at what he sees.*]

JOHN. Winston? What's happening? Why are you punishing me?

WINSTON [*quietly*]. You stink, John. You stink of beer, of company, of *poes*, of freedom. . . . Your freedom stinks, John, and it's driving me mad.

JOHN. No, Winston!

WINSTON. Yes! Don't deny it. Three months time, at this hour, you'll be wiping beer off your face, your hands on your balls, and *poes* waiting for you. You will laugh, you will drink, you will fuck and forget.

[*John's denials have no effect on Winston.*]

Stop bullshitting me! We've got no time left for that. There's only two months left between us. [*Pause.*] You know where I ended up this morning, John? In the quarry. Next to old Harry. Do you know old Harry, John?

JOHN. Yes.

WINSTON. Yes what? Speak, man!

JOHN. Old Harry, Cell Twenty-three, seventy years, serving Life!

WINSTON. That's not what I'm talking about. When you go to the quarry tomorrow, take a good look at old Harry. Look into his eyes, John. Look at his hands. They've changed him. They've turned him into stone. Watch him work with that chisel and hammer. Twenty perfect blocks of stone every day. Nobody else can do it like him. He loves stone. That's why they're nice to him. He's forgotten himself. He's forgotten everything . . . why he's here, where he comes from.

That's happening to me John. I've forgotten why I'm here.

71

JOHN. No.

WINSTON. Why am I here?

JOHN. You put your head on the block for others.

WINSTON. Fuck the others.

JOHN. Don't say that! Remember our ideals. . . .

WINSTON. Fuck our ideals. . . .

JOHN. No Winston . . . our slogans, our children's freedom. . . .

WINSTON. Fuck slogans, fuck politics . . . fuck everything, John. Why am I here? I'm jealous of your freedom, John. I also want to count. God also gave me ten fingers, but what do I count? My life? How do I count it, John? One . . . one . . . another day comes . . . one. . . . Help me, John! . . . Another day . . . one . . . one. . . . Help me, brother! . . . one. . . .

[*John has sunk to the floor, helpless in the face of the other man's torment and pain. Winston almost seems to bend under the weight of the life stretching ahead of him on the Island. For a few seconds he lives in silence with his reality, then slowly straightens up. He turns and looks at John. When he speaks again, it is the voice of a man who has come to terms with his fate, massively compassionate.*]

Nyana we Sizwe!

[*John looks up at him.*]

Nyana we Sizwe . . . it's all over now. All over. [*He moves over to John.*] Forget me. . . .

[*John attempts a last, limp denial.*]

No, John! Forget me . . . because I'm going to forget you. Yes, I will forget you. Others will come in here, John, count, go, and I'll forget them. Still more will come, count like you, go like you, and I will forget them. And then one day, it will all be over.

[*A lighting change suggests the passage of time. Winston collects together their props for Antigone.*]

Come. They're waiting.

JOHN. Do you know your words?

WINSTON. Yes. Come, we'll be late for the concert.

SCENE FOUR

The two men convert their cell-area into a stage for the prison concert. Their blankets are hung to provide a makeshift backdrop behind which Winston disappears with their props. John comes forward and addresses the audience. He is not yet in his Creon costume.

JOHN. Captain Prinsloo, Hodoshe, Warders, . . . and Gentlemen! Two brothers of the House of Labdacus found themselves on opposite sides in battle, the one defending the State, the other attacking it. They both died on the battlefield. King Creon, Head of the State, decided that the one who had defended the State would be buried with all religious rites due to the noble dead. But the other one, the traitor Polynices, who had come back from exile intending to burn and destroy his fatherland, to drink the blood of his masters, was to have no grave, no mourning. He was to lie on the open fields to rot, or at most be food for the jackals. It was a law. But Antigone, their sister, defied the law and buried the body of her brother Polynices. She was caught and arrested. That is why tonight the Hodoshe Span, Cell Forty-two, presents for your entertainment: 'The Trial and Punishment of Antigone'.

[*He disappears behind the blankets. They simulate a fanfare of trumpets. At its height the blankets open and he steps out as Creon. In addition to his pendant, there is some sort of crown and a blanket draped over his shoulders as a robe.*]

My People! Creon stands before his palace and greets you! Stop! Stop! What's that I hear? You, good man, speak up. Did I hear 'Hail the King'? My good people, I am your *servant* . . . a happy one, but still your servant. How many times must I ask you, implore you to see in these symbols of office nothing more, or less, than you would in the uniform of the humblest menial in your house. Creon's crown is as simple, and I hope as clean, as the apron Nanny wears. And even as Nanny smiles and is your happy servant because she sees her charge . . . your child! . . . waxing fat in that little cradle, so too does Creon—your obedient servant!—stand here and smile. For what does he see? Fatness and happiness! How else does

73

one measure the success of a state? By the sumptuousness of the palaces built for its king and princes? The magnificence of the temples erected to its gods? The achievements of its scientists and technicians who can now send rockets to the moon? No! These count for nothing beside the fatness and happiness of its people.

But have you ever paused to ask yourself whose responsibility it is to maintain that fatness and happiness? The answer is simple, is it not? . . . your servant the king! But have you then gone on to ask yourself what does the king need to maintain this happy state of affairs? What, other than his silly crown, are the tools with which a king fashions the happiness of his people? The answer is equally simple, my good people. The law! Yes. The law. A three-lettered word, and how many times haven't you glibly used it, never bothering to ask yourselves, 'What then is the law?' Or if you have, then making recourse to such clichés as 'the law states this . . . or the law states that'. The law states or maintains nothing, good people. The law defends! The law is no more or less than a shield in your faithful servant's hand to protect YOU! But even as a shield would be useless in one hand, to defend, without a sword in the other, to strike . . . so too the law has its edge. The penalty! We have come through difficult times. I am sure it is needless for me to remind you of the constant troubles on our borders . . . those despicable rats who would gnaw away at our fatness and happiness. We have been diligent in dealing with them. But unfortunately there are still at large subversive elements . . . there are still amongst us a few rats that are not satisfied and to them I must show this face of Creon . . . so different to the one that hails my happy people! It is with a heavy heart, and you shall see why soon enough, that I must tell you that we have caught another one. That is why I have assembled you here. Let what follows be a living lesson for those among you misguided enough still to harbour sympathy for rats! The shield has defended. Now the sword must strike!

Bring in the accused.

[*Winston, dressed as Antigone, enters. He wears the wig, the necklace of nails, and a blanket around his waist as a skirt.*]

Your name!

WINSTON. Antigone, daughter of Oedipus, sister of Eteocles and Polynices.

JOHN. You are accused that, in defiance of the law, you buried the body of the traitor Polynices.

WINSTON. I buried the body of my brother Polynices.

JOHN. Did you know there was a law forbidding that?

WINSTON. Yes.

JOHN. Yet you defied it.

WINSTON. Yes.

JOHN. Did you know the consequences of such defiance?

WINSTON. Yes.

JOHN. What did you plead to the charges laid against you? Guilty or Not Guilty?

WINSTON. Guilty.

JOHN. Antigone, you have pleaded guilty. Is there anything you wish to say in mitigation? This is your last chance. Speak.

WINSTON. Who made the law forbidding the burial of my brother?

JOHN. The State.

WINSTON. Who is the State?

JOHN. As King I am its manifest symbol.

WINSTON. So you made the law.

JOHN. Yes, for the State.

WINSTON. Are you God?

JOHN. Watch your words, little girl!

WINSTON. You said it was my chance to speak.

JOHN. But not to ridicule.

WINSTON. I've got no time to waste on that. Your sentence on my life hangs waiting on your lips.

JOHN. Then speak on.

WINSTON. When Polynices died in battle, all that remained was the empty husk of his body. He could neither harm nor help any man again. What lay on the battlefield waiting for Hodoshe to turn rotten, belonged to God. You are only a man, Creon. Even as there are laws made by men, so too there are others that come from God. He watches my soul for a

75

transgression even as your spies hide in the bush at night to see who is transgressing your laws. Guilty against God I will not be for any man on this earth. Even without your law, Creon, and the threat of death to whoever defied it, I know I must die. Because of your law and my defiance, that fate is now very near. So much the better. Your threat is nothing to me, Creon. But if I had let my mother's son, a Son of the Land, lie there as food for the carrion fly, Hodoshe, my soul would never have known peace. Do you understand anything of what I am saying, Creon?

JOHN. Your words reveal only that obstinacy of spirit which has brought nothing but tragedy to your people. First you break the law. Now you insult the State.

WINSTON. Just because I ask you to remember that you are only a man?

JOHN. And to add insult to injury you gloat over your deeds! No, Antigone, you will not escape with impunity. Were you my own child you would not escape full punishment.

WINSTON. Full punishment? Would you like to do more than just kill me?

JOHN. That is all I wish.

WINSTON. Then let us not waste any time. Stop talking. I buried my brother. That is an honourable thing, Creon. All these people in your state would say so too, if fear of you and another law did not force them into silence.

JOHN. You are wrong. None of my people think the way you do.

WINSTON. Yes they do, but no one dares tell you so. You will not sleep peacefully, Creon.

JOHN. You add shamelessness to your crimes, Antigone.

WINSTON. I do not feel any shame at having honoured my brother.

JOHN. Was he that died with him not also your brother?

WINSTON. He was.

JOHN. And so you honour the one and insult the other.

WINSTON. I shared my love, not my hate.

JOHN. Go then and share your love among the dead. I will have no rats' law here while yet I live.

76

WINSTON. We are wasting time, Creon. Stop talking. Your words defeat your purpose. They are prolonging my life.

JOHN [*again addressing the audience*]. You have heard all the relevant facts. Needless now to call the state witnesses who would testify beyond reasonable doubt that the accused is guilty. Nor, for that matter, is it in the best interests of the State to disclose their identity. There was a law. The law was broken. The law stipulated its penalty. My hands are tied.

Take her from where she stands, straight to the Island! There wall her up in a cell for life, with enough food to acquit ourselves of the taint of her blood.

WINSTON [*to the audience*]. Brothers and Sisters of the Land! I go now on my last journey. I must leave the light of day forever, for the Island, strange and cold, to be lost between life and death. So, to my grave, my everlasting prison, condemned alive to solitary death.

[*Tearing off his wig and confronting the audience as Winston, not Antigone.*]

Gods of our Fathers! My Land! My Home!

Time waits no longer. I go now to my living death, because I honoured those things to which honour belongs.

[*The two men take off their costumes and then strike their 'set'. They then come together and, as in the beginning, their hands come together to suggest handcuffs, and their right and left legs to suggest ankle-chains. They start running . . . John mumbling a prayer, and Winston a rhythm for their three-legged run.*
The siren wails.
Fade to blackout.]

77

GLOSSARY

ag voetsek: go to hell
bioscope: cinema
broer: brother
Ciskei *(adj.* Ciskeian):   one of the Black 'homelands' created by the South African Government under its policy of Separate Development
dankie: thank you
gqokra izi khuselo zamehlo kule ndawo: put on safety glasses here
hai; haai: exclamation of surprise
hier is ek: here I am
ja: yes
kieries: fighting-sticks carried by young African men
lap; lappie: rag
makulu: grandmother
moer: literally, womb; used as a swear-word equivalent to 'fuck', 'fucking'
nyana we sizwe: brother of the land
ons was gemoer vandag: we were fucked up today
poes: cunt
tshotsholoza kulezondawo, vyabaleka: opening phrase of an African work-chant; literally, work steady, the train is coming
tsotsis: Black hooligans